I0621934

What May Come of Our Darkness

a series of short stories
by Robin Anne Ettles

Copyright © 2019 Robin Anne Ettles.

leftbranching@gmail.com

All rights reserved. No part of this book may be reproduced, stored, or transmitted by any means—whether auditory, graphic, mechanical, or electronic—without written permission of the author, except in the case of brief excerpts used in critical articles and reviews. Unauthorized reproduction of any part of this work is illegal and is punishable by law.

This is a work of fiction. All of the characters, names, incidents, organizations, and dialogue in this novel are either the products of the author's imagination or are used fictitiously.

ISBN: 978-1-9994630-0-7 (sc)
ISBN: 978-1-9994630-1-4 (e)

Cover image: © Robin Anne Ettles.

Author image by Jared Doyle.

Because of the dynamic nature of the Internet, any web addresses or links contained in this book may have changed since publication and may no longer be valid. The views expressed in this work are solely those of the author and do not necessarily reflect the views of the publisher, and the publisher hereby disclaims any responsibility for them.

Any people depicted in stock imagery provided by Getty Images are models, and such images are being used for illustrative purposes only. Certain stock imagery © Getty Images.

Lulu Publishing Services rev. date: 01/09/2019

Contents

Gerry and Cody Watts Were on Their Way Home

Gerry and Cody Watts were on their way home from an impromptu gathering in Mike Howard's work shed.

They had gone up to return a few tools they had borrowed to shore up the back door of their small and old house, and had brought Mike some rum as a token of their appreciation. Father and son both hoped Mike would do what he normally did when presented with a bottle: receive it with one hand, crack it open with the other, and release his inner performer about halfway through. He didn't disappoint.

Neither did Matt, who didn't feel like watching Sportsnet anymore while being subjected to the background noise of his wife's perpetual telephone conversation with her best and most gossipy friend. Matt showed up at Mike's with beer and a list of "holy faaaawk"s a mile long, providing easy fodder for The Mike Show.

Derrick and his new girlfriend, without whom he was never seen these days, also dropped by. It was felt that Derrick was rather proud of having netted one of the most beautiful girls in the community, who was, in fact, one of the most beautiful girls any of them had ever seen. No one complained when he stopped arriving solo.

Seeing the number of cars in the yard right off the highway, Evan, Morrison, and Jake pulled in. They were as high as kites, which was convenient, as they wouldn't eradicate the entire supply of beer. As darkness fell with late autumn quickness, fifteen people were packed into the shed. Mike let the fire go out and opened the windows. While he provided most of the entertainment via his stories from the new hotel worksite down by the wharf, with occasional picks at Poor Matt, there were many spinoff conversations and laughs. The gathering got louder by the hour.

Gerry poked his son suddenly. He leaned in and said, "We gotta go."

Cody was about to protest. He had just opened another beer. He was also having some degree of fun for the first time in months. Things at the steel plant had been heated lately. To say that he didn't get along with his new supervisor was a miserable understatement. Cody did not tend to torch one relationship at a time; when things lit up, everyone and everything in proximity got seared. He was on the brink of unemployment. He was ignoring calls from Revenue Canada regarding the last five years of unfiled income tax. He was recovering from a broken foot and had just gotten through his first week free of crutches. The second anniversary of his mother's death was three days fresh.

His flash of protest was instantly doused by the thought of his father, drunk. There was nothing good about that. Nothing good at all. His father's alarm was also his own. After ten years of sobriety, Gerry had begun dipping into the odd drink or two. Nothing had gone awry yet. But Gerry knew when the fever was about to hit, and he and his son had an unwavering consensus that when Gerry gave the signal, they were out. Gerry didn't recall much from his drinking days. Instead, he retained a paralyzing physical and emotional memory of the awfulness he had caused his family. Friends. Strangers.

"What? Gerry, no. Come on, Gerry!" drawled Mike, gesturing grandly.

"Early day tomorrow. That doorframe won't pay for itself. Thanks for the loaners — you're a star." Gerry sidled his giant, awkward self through friends and acquaintances and met Cody, who, despite the tender foot, was already standing at the door.

The few who registered the departure said goodbye. The others carried on, absorbed in their conversations and laughter, buzzed out, oblivious, lost in fun.

The chill of the evening snapped father and son back into the world outside the shed. The father was grateful for the mild shock. It pulled the cravings from the centre of his belly out through the tendons of his hands and lifted them away, like the frost rising from their breath.

"Cocksuckin' winter," growled the son, who, by contrast, felt himself tense against the cold. The two walked past a pile of abandoned dirtbikes, their twisted frames lying at odd angles. The alarming, stained foam innards of ripped seats were lit garishly by the flood-light at the apex of the shed. "Jesus. Look at that waste. He'll never do nothin' with that."

"Not likely," said Gerry. He decided to take what was his Step 2 of distancing himself from his cravings: Make Someone Laugh. "Derrick did pretty good, wha? Nice face, too."

"Jesus, Dad, shu-ddup," said Cody, shaking his head in disgust, trying to dismiss the mental image of his father appraising a girl his own age. "Gaaahh."

Gerry grinned slightly. Each opened a front door of Gerry's car and fell onto opposite sides of the bench seat. "Gaaahhh!" said Cody again, more emphatically, a laugh forming at the tail end of his dismay.

Neither of them minded Gerry's twenty-year-old Crown Vic. It fit Big Gerry. It had a calming effect on Cody, who, slim and wiry, could stretch out and enjoy what felt like floating down the highway. Plus, Gerry's insistence on keeping the Vic running allowed Cody to own a truck. It was Cody's prized possession. It got him to and from his shitty job, and was the only thing that provided him with enough motivation to stop just short of getting fired on a daily basis.

They set off on the dark, two-lane highway, made darker than usual by the heavily overcast sky. Cody leaned back and, three beers and a snort of rum in, gave himself over to the Vic's gentle ride toward their home.

The Watts boys were not roommates out of any genuine desire for the arrangement. The guise was that neither of them made enough money to step out on their own. Neither of them had met a new lady worthy of a change in domestic arrangements. The unspoken truth was that if they parted ways, they were finally both fully parted from Leah. Despite the frequent tensions between them, this was not an option.

In Cody's repertoire of family facts, neither of them had met a new lady at all since his mother's death. His version of family facts was not mirrored by Gerry's. But what his son didn't know yet wouldn't hurt either of them. They weren't ready. The deliberate silence of Gerry's new relationship wouldn't hurt anyone at all.

Father and son chatted back and forth about the evening. They laughed about Poor Matt, who didn't notice for one second how badly Mike had been ribbing him. Cody talked about how he wished Jake wasn't such a goddamn snake, because he'd start an engine repair business with Jake in a heartbeat, if Jake could ever say what he meant or mean what he said.

They rounded an S-curve in the road between Nicholson's farm and the marsh. Cody let himself close his eyes for a fraction of a second and heard the engine rev.

"Shit," his father said. Then, alarmingly: "Shit. SHIT. SHIT. HANG ON–"

Something had let go. Gerry stomped madly on the brake pedal, sending it repeatedly to the floor like a sewing machine needle. He snapped the gear shift into neutral but all control was gone. As the car bolted directly for the deep marsh on the left, Gerry spun the wheel. Cody, wearing no seat belt, flew across the bench seat and into his father. The car caught a terrible angle in the opposite ditch, throwing Cody away from his father and through the passenger window. Then, the car slowly flipped, twisted, and slammed down onto its right side.

The silence was terrible. Through it, Gerry finally heard his son's voice, whispering, "Dad Dad Dad Dad Dad ... Dad ... Dad Dad ... Dad ... Dad ... Dad ..."

Gerry's eyes were open wider than they had ever been. He slowly turned to his right and bent his neck as much as he could toward Cody's voice, where he only saw the upper half of son through the space where the window had been. Cody's lower half was crushed under the weight of the car. "Dad ... Dad ... Dad ... I can't ... breathe ... Dad ... Dadhands"

Gerry felt his head turn slowly back toward the steering wheel, which was wedged between his spread legs. One of them was cut deeply where the wheel had sunk into it. The dashboard was folded in half. He saw slow movement, liquid, falling in the direction of his son. He raised his eyes inch by inch to see his hands dangling from their wrists, and twin rivers of blood flowing more darkly than the night itself from the abrupt ends of his arms.

There was no tunnel. There was no fading light.

The light simply went out.

Dims

Dims didn't much care for being called Dims. His name was Dimitri. His half-Russian father clung deeply to any concept that made his family not run-of-the-mill, and had named all three of his children accordingly. Dimitri's seventh grade classmates had re-baptized him Dims. The nickname was not an improvement. In general, Dims did not feel that he had much going for him. What he had instead was a terrible time learning; a shyness that bordered on mutism; middle-child birth order; and a set of hippie parents who didn't have two social cues to rub together.

His mother seemed oblivious to life outside of their house, which she refused to leave. She claimed the extra weight of her slight figure in the car engendered unnecessary consumption. She was also extremely busy rebatching and upcycling and macrobiologizing and making all of her oldest daughter's clothes and then handing them down to her youngest son.

Yelena was a full-figured girl; her clothes were out for Dims, whose build took after their mother's. Boris, the younger boy, was quite portly. By default, he inherited most of Yelena's clothes, altered in the places that mattered. Dims felt great relief for himself but sheer mortification for his brother. Boris, however, portrayed unwavering nonchalance.

No one in the family could understand how Boris was significantly wider than the rest of them. It certainly wasn't genetics, or the family's financially lean diet. Meanwhile, Dims had chosen to remain silent about his recent discovery of Boris's job in the school cafeteria. The job allowed Boris to feast on fries daily. One of the doting older ladies washed his uniform and hat, so he never smelled of grease.

Then there was the unsolved theft of tech items and lunches from numerous school lockers. One night, Dims opened his brother's bookbag in hopes of finding some extra graph paper. Instead, he found a set of lime green earbuds that he had seen on his own classmate, Jonah, whom Dims didn't like very much. Dims re-set the contents and folds of the bookbag exactly as he had found them. He suddenly had an explanation for his brother's nonchalance about the hand-me-downs, and about everything else, for that matter: Boris was laying low.

The various ways in which the Kozlovs went noticed and unnoticed became highly altered on the day of Dim's year-end school field trip.

Dims had been excited about the field trip in a much different way than his classmates. He planned to get off the bus at the harbourfront and disappear until ten minutes before departure, at which time he would reappear early, much to the praise of the chaperone staff. A perfect day lay ahead of him, alone in town.

The buses lurched to a stop. Kids descended excitedly. Dims blended into the melee as it mixed in with pedestrian traffic. He ducked behind buildings and benches, and watched as the rest of the students headed for the fun park.

Confident the coast was clear and his absence overlooked, Dims rose from behind a sandwich board and attempted what he hoped resembled his brother's indifference. He strolled with an overly casual swagger through the downtown core. He walked among groups of tourists. He stopped and flipped through a pile of marked-down CDs at a used record store. He sat on the steps of the town hall and watched the world go by.

Not surprisingly, no one in the Kozlov family had ever been issued a watch. Dims tensed suddenly, feeling the approach of the departure time. He started off in a flailing power walk. Finding this too remarkable, he slowed his pace to what he thought was an easy gait, but then felt like he was limping in slow motion. He tried normal walking. This no longer felt normal. He found himself physically confused.

To check the time, Dims stepped back into the record store, where, earlier, he had noticed a giant clock in the style of Flavor Flav occupying one of the walls. As he turned to leave, the sound of a confrontation at the back of the store caught his attention. Two employees charged from behind the cash, hollering as they dove to the ground, presumably to catch a shoplifter.

The employees, one guy and one girl, rose awkwardly on either side of 16-year-old Yelena Kozlov. "You've totally got this wrong and you're in major shit!" barked Yelena.

"Security video disagrees," said the girl employee. "How about you spare everyone further embarrassment and dump the CDs out of your pants?"

Oh God, thought Dims. He realized that he had been entirely unnoticed by the staff and his sister, and prepared to run. He paused briefly and looked up. A camera looked straight back down at him.

Ohhhhhh God, thought Dims. Assume nonchalance! he thought. Become Boris! No. Become an actor! He tilted his head, shook it slowly and somewhat dramatically for the benefit of the camera, and walked off with excessive middle school self-assurance toward the office behind the cash.

The office walls had been plastered years ago with old, damaged record covers and rotting posters for bands he had never heard of. The air was devoid of movement or freshness. The guy employee spoke with the police while the girl employee blocked Yelena's exit. Yelena paced. "Fucking idiots!" she hissed. "You have no right to do this. You have NO idea who my father is! You'll be so – fucking – SORRY"

Her voice caught as she saw Dims in the doorway. "Who the fuck are you??" she yelled, fully committed to her own volatility and expansive manner of improv.

Who exactly does she think our father is? thought Dims. He snapped back to the scenario at hand. "I ... uh ... I was ... looking for some classical music," he said, in a voice he barely recognized. He began to sweat profusely.

Yelena was clearly dying to comment on her brother's performance, but compromised with her already compromising situation by remaining silent.

The girl employee looked at him, stone-faced. "Classical music."

"Yeah," said Dims, with mild indignation.

"What composer were you looking for?"

"Composer," repeated Dims, nodding slowly. "Yes." A bizarre silence followed.

"OH MY GOD" hollered Yelena at the ceiling, abruptly terminating one of her better attempts at self-control. "This is my stupid little brother." She gnashed her teeth together and thrust her neck out toward Dims. "Ffffsssssshidiot!"

The guy employee had ended the call. "This true?" he asked Dims.

Dims looked down and didn't reply. His improv skills were badly in need of work.

My perfect day, thought Dims. The thick and terrible anxiety that had been growing inside of him now reached an odd point of tolerability. He became more aware of his disastrous surroundings. My perfect day is gone.

All four individuals stood or sat in various positions around the airless office for what seemed like a long time. Finally, two police cars pulled up in front of the store. The guy employee jumped from the desk. "Yes!" he proclaimed.

"Worst. Shift. Ever," muttered the girl employee.

Two cars? Dims and Yelena thought separately.

Two officers got out of the first car and went around to the back door. They removed Erik Kozlov, who, while not in handcuffs, was escorted into the store very much as if he was. Both children regarded their father with curiosity and concern. The party reached the doorway. Erik stepped slightly forward.

"We are all being taken to the police station," he said commandingly, in a pre-scripted way. We're all actors today! thought Dimitri.

The officers stood still and silent. During the length of time between the initial phone call to police and the arrival of police and parent, which, ordinarily, should not have taken three hours, a great deal of information had come to light about the Kozlov family. Erik's speech to his children had clearly been negotiated prior to his arrival at the record store. He continued.

"There are some things you need to know first. The gentlemen behind me believe in taxes, and I don't, so, there's that. And – " his caught his breath, then continued. "Your mother has been arrested separately, on charges that were initially related to drugs. She won't be home for a while. She – I mean, we – did some – I mean, a lot – of things a few years ago that we really aren't proud of. You need to know that we don't blame you for this coming out today." He looked directly at Yelena.

What, thought Dims, is happening.

"You will probably be staying with another family for a bit," Erik now pushed through his emotionality, looking at his son. Dims could hear his sister's voice rising as she said the word "no" over and over. Their father cleared his throat and regained his deliberate tone of authority. "It won't be forever, and you will be cared for, and I will come for you."

With the last phrase, Dims wondered if anyone could see his stomach descending through his shoes with the weight of his father's lie.

In the back of the second police car, Yelena tried and failed to get herself under control. Seated beside her, Dims watched as their father's head was ducked into the back of the car ahead of them. The police talked at some length with the employees and took notes. People had gathered. At least it's much cooler in here, thought Dims. Then both vehicles pulled away.

Several hours later, Dims was directed into the backseat of a normal car. He was driven to a brick building where he was joined by Boris, nonchalant as always. Neither spoke as they were taken to a suburban home and accompanied to the front door under the twilight sky. They sat very still in a living room with plump furniture and impeccably clean lamps and fixtures while the adults chatted. The brothers were eventually escorted by a friendly and smiling older couple down to a large bedroom in the basement. A set of twin beds was squared against opposing walls.

The bedroom had never held children of the couple's own conception, despite their earnest dreams and efforts. Instead, it had become a vessel for the haunted dreams and transient safety of many other children prior to Dimitri and Boris Kozlov.

Dims went over and over the events of the day as the brothers lay on opposite sides of the room with the lights out. So many things now made sense; so many more made none. He gazed around the room from his horizontal perspective. There were identical desks and dressers, and a closet with doors. The streetlight, diffused by the window's sheer curtains, illuminated everything in a friendly, proximate way. It was a quality of light that had you know other people were close; probably nice people, like the couple who owned the house. The room smelled clean. The sheets smelled fresh. Dims could make out the lines of overly vigilant vacuuming embedded in the white carpet beneath them. He was surprised by the unexpected emotion of comfort.

"It'll be ok," were the first words he had said in hours, directed to the sole audience of his little brother Boris. They were the first encouraging or authentic words he had spoken in a long time.

Boris said nothing. Dims imagined sleep, or pre-sleep nonchalance, over in the bed across the way of the clean carpet. Then he heard the sound of quiet crying.

The Price of Admission

Amy's home and refuge was a small, hot, stuffy, upper floor, no-real-fire-escape studio apartment in a building circa 1930 off an alley that was once a street off a side street not far from Dundas Square. She had done a brilliant job of arranging the tiny space, and was a decent housekeeper. This resulted in some degree of aesthetic and ideological dissonance relative to the overall state of the building itself, whose interior and exterior appearance were in severe decline. Over the years, her highly conscientious latino and / or elderly neighbours had disappeared, and somehow re-emerged as mostly white hipsters.

They weren't interesting hipsters, either. They talked at length about profound films they were going to make. They never made any. They drank Pabst Blue Ribbon and thought themselves very cultured. Their philosophy of sharing meant that they didn't really have anything of their own, so they used yours. While she had never socialized much with her previous neighbours, Amy preferred their variety of distal company, and had felt far more comfortable around them. Over time, her home had come to consist exclusively of the small box beyond her numbered apartment door. The hallways and stairways and entryways all felt like they belonged to the hipsters in a building they didn't own.

Amy wasn't much of a drinker, so it worked out well for them when she politely refused their reluctant offers of beer in exchange for some flour, rice, batteries, vegan egg whites, kimchi. She still shook her head at the thought of the last items. Her initially open spirit and curiosity toward them shut down quickly. She began to ignore the knocks at the door. It only took a few minutes before they would go away, and about three months for them to stop knocking altogether. She sensed when they were around; she sensed no danger from them. In person, they remained polite, as hipsters are wont to be. They smiled and readily exchanged friendly 'heys' with Amy when their paths would cross. If they called her a miser or a recluse or a weirdo, she never heard them. Also, they were clearly getting their needs met elsewhere.

She wasn't sure if they worked, or went to school, or were doled out spare change from trust funds, or some combination of these. Amy herself did not work currently. She quit the University of Toronto in 2000 but kept the apartment she had lived in during school. There was no trust fund. However, a recent and unexpected inheritance received from the estate of an aunt with whom Amy hadn't spoken in decades would carry Amy a full year, if she was smart. A full year to decide what she would do next, even though she had spent the previous year deciding what she would do next. When the first year of deciding rolled into the second, it became clear that her decision had been to maintain a holding pattern of deciding nothing in particular.

She was three months into year two.

The shocking sum had been deposited into her account nearly six months previously. Amy recalled liking her aunt quite a bit. The memories were fond but definitely far, at least for Amy. The aunt had obviously kept her sentiments from their time together much closer to her heart and, subsequently, to her final wishes. Amy's shock rolled into guilt which rolled into physically unbearable excitement which rolled back into guilt and then into relief. It took weeks for the emotions to abate. It was exhausting. During the initial roller coaster of affect following the anomalous bank statement, Amy did a pile of math and pacing, and reserved money for the habit she had been on the brink of no longer being able to afford: a membership pass at the Toronto Aquarium.

Three-quarters of a science degree was not the most employable of assets. She had worked a number of semi-menial jobs after choosing to not return for her graduating year. Her very last job was that of data entry for a high-profile accounting firm. She was exceptionally efficient, discreet, and decently paid. Her supervisor seemed to feel that she would return to school someday, and he was fully supportive in this regard. He did not whatsoever anticipate that on Wednesday, October 29, he would say goodbye to the back of her as she raised her hand in a wave on her way out, never to see any side of her ever again.

This day had been coming since late August, when Amy had woken one day and felt highly uncomfortable about going to work, in the exact way she had woken one day and felt highly uncomfortable about going back for her fourth year of university. However, unlike what happened with university, she got up and went to work. She came home. The prickly, weighty feeling was there with her the next day, and the next, and each day she woke and was due in to work. She went about the rest of her life quite functionally, although she found herself spending more and more time at home. She recalled that it was the day before Halloween when she opened her eyes one day and her first thought was: ENOUGH. She lay in bed staring at the grey ceiling until noon. She never called in. Her phone later indicated that a number from work had called a few times, as well as her parents. Dots were eventually connected somewhere outside of her apartment, resulting in two city police officers arriving on her doorstep. I'm fine, she said. Just done. They stepped forward three short feet into her living room / bedroom, and gently and kindly asked the obligatory mental health assessment questions. They listened to what were perfectly acceptable responses within the parameters of their training. They wished her a good day, and left.

It was a week before she touched her computer; another before she left the apartment, which was a forced outing on account of having creatively consumed every ounce of the contents of her cupboards and refrigerator.

Despite her discomfort as she descended the stairs and opened the main door, she was surprised by how something was entirely different as she walked out into full daylight. The world seemed different to her; fresher. The city seemed less hostile and unclean. The pace of her breathing slowed. In the days and weeks to come, she found herself at peace with the absence of active human interaction, interrupted only by exchanges with store clerks. She stopped using her phone as a phone pretty much altogether, and maintained superficial connections with friends via text and social media. I'm fine, she responded through text if they asked by text. Just done. Trying to figure out what I'm actually supposed to be doing.

The Toronto Aquarium was a place she had never visited during her time in the city until about 3 months into her new world of on-going unemployment. She had established a ritual of going to a museum or art gallery every week or so. Then art started to bore her, which was an unwelcome feeling. This feeling eventually demanded acknowledgement, so she began surfing the internet for things-to-see-and-do-in-Toronto. "Destinations" such as the beach or Toronto Island were out for her; she had vacationed with her family in nice places with nice beaches, and couldn't seriously agree with Toronto's idea of a beach. The aquarium came up frequently while she surfed. She stopped ignoring the suggestion. Aquarium it was.

Something absolutely new to Amy awoke inside of her as she surveyed creatures of all manner of shape, size, colour, and strangeness moving about in their artificially reconstructed worlds beyond the glass walls. She gently shuffled backward along the slow conveyor belt so she could remain in place and get a better grasp of the moving images all around and above her. In Amy's mind and heart, it was as though her studies in biology and the appreciation of colour and form she had gained through painting had become one beautiful thing. She saw the brilliant blues and greens; sharp silver scales, and even sharper eyes. She saw the mirror of their oxygen use, critical on one side of the glass and fatal on the other. She saw electromagnetic perception flowing in unidirectional chains of prey. She saw gender roles executed in unconventional and peaceful practicality. The discovery of this ever-moving visual and intellectual masterpiece made her feel calm and at home. She bought a membership pass. She made changes to her budget as necessary to accommodate the cost.

While never at the same time, she went to the aquarium almost every day for several weeks, and let the creatures make their incredible moving art for her.

Over time, the direction of her attention shifted slightly. She also began to observe the movement of tourists, locals, families, kids on school outings.

On account of her inconsistent visiting times, it took a while for her to spot the returning clientele. Their variety was refreshing and intriguing relative to the narrow, predictable bandwidth of museum and gallery dwellers. Visitors to the aquarium hailed from all socioeconomic backgrounds, and allowed themselves to show their delight more freely.

One week, she went at 3 p.m. on a Monday. She happened to notice a man of about her age, in his early 30s. There was something familiar about him that she couldn't place. After thinking about it for a while as she strolled and surveyed, she understood that the sense of familiarity was caused by his prototypicality. He had slightly messy hair, deliberately maintained three-day scruff, and was neither fit nor unfit. He was dressed decently but understatedly, wore a small man purse strapped across his back, and held onto a travel mug. Amy was curious about her curiosity toward another individual, yet not altogether surprised by it. It had been some time since she had bothered with the inevitably messy and highly unpredictable effort of metro area dating. She returned home to routine later that afternoon and didn't think too much about the man until the next Monday, when she feebly fought the urge to return to the aquarium precisely at 3 p.m., and failed.

This pattern was repeated the following Monday. It was broken the Monday after that. Their paths finally crossed within the depths of the lower floor, where they exchanged smiles, and chose to approach.

"Amy," her voice said. Her voice was rich in its sound, and she was mildly taken aback by it. She had not addressed another human being out of personal interest in some time.

"Jared," he replied. "It's nice to finally meet you."

"Coffee?" she asked, not remotely attempting to hide her own surprise as she immediately advanced the communication.

"Yeah," he said with a warm laugh.

"Let's get out of here."

At a nearby café of Jared's choosing, the So-what-are-we-each-doing-spending-so-much-time-at-an-aquarium question was met with highly parallel answers. Both were bored of visual art for purposes of entertainment and culture. Neither of them liked theatre very much. Jared turned out to like movies a lot more than Amy did.

The Where-did-all-this-time-come-from-to-hang-out-at-an-aquarium question was met with prepared answers. The tone of their new acquaintanceship shifted slightly. Both Jared and Amy had experienced the truth-lies continuum on which one's personal history was conveyed among strangers. For each of them, the discomfort of certain aspects of their personal history was still somewhat raw. But each of their carapace had grown, and they moved forward with their responses.

"I came into some money," said Amy. She instantly grit her teeth and shook her head. "That's not quite how it sounds, actually. I know it sounds terrible. I live in a tiny apartment in a shit building that I've been in for 14 years because I like the neighbourhood. I've not liked a single job I've held. I've been given the strange gift of an extra year to just be and figure some things out. That's a major privilege, really," she said, meaning for her last sentence in particular to be true.

"Huh," he said. Whatever he was thinking in that moment was followed outwardly with a nod and a sincere, "That's great."

"You?" she asked without pause. She heard the rate of her own speech, and, this time, tried not to appear startled by it. There had been some detrimental effect on her social skills from prolonged absence from real conversation.

"Well," he said, willing himself to maintain eye contact, "I got fired close to a year ago. I went to work high one day. One day. One day, I went to work, high. That day also turned out to be random drug test day. I had forgotten that I had signed a waiver when I first started the job with a clause about random drug testing, which I was told would likely never happen, and which had never happened once in six years. I was as high as a guy could be. I'd not touched recreational drugs for years prior to that. Wasn't my thing. And I've not been high since."

"High on what?" Jesus, give him some space, she thought. She couldn't.

Jared's level of practiced concentration overrode the impetus of her questioning. "Blow." he said. "Just before heading into a night shift in annual series of several, where we'd back up and clean up servers for a market research company. I'd been vacuuming my apartment before I headed out that evening and found some stuff that someone must have accidentally left behind the weekend before. I went to chuck it, and was, like, screw it. Why not. It'll make the night more amusing."

"You wound up throwing a lot away," she said immediately, yet compassionately.

Jared paused. The moment of confession had passed, and the tone of her response had lightened him. He raised his hands in a friendly, mocking surrender. "I did throw a lot away. But I'm totally owning all of this magic right here."

Amy smiled back, but felt paled by the level of sincerity he had chosen to offer relative to her own. She was simultaneously repulsed by the drug use, even if his honestly regarding his prior lack of drug use did, in fact, extend "for years." Her internal organs shut down a little in their excitement. She knew they would only be friends. The cooling feeling at the table was mutual, and accompanied by a sense of relief. A friend. This idea seemed novel to both of them, and possibly nice.

They let the dust of the recent past settle, and chatted their way back further into their lives. They found some common ground in suburban upbringing and post-secondary education; childhood friends with whom they had managed to keep some connection via social media; early participation in lots of sports. A couple of hours had passed, of which they became aware in the same moment. "Next Monday?" he asked, with a smile that seemed to come from his heart rather than from his mouth. He was good at smiling. Amy found that it felt good to be smiled at.

Amy returned this, with little effort. "Next Monday."

A couple of Mondays came and went, quite pleasantly. There was a fair amount of silence, which both appreciated, particularly Amy.

In the speaking portion of their time together, they learned more about one another. Amy learned that Jared frequented the aquarium on Mondays as this was his consistent day off. Jared's younger brother had demonstrated zero loss of faith in Jared after his misstep, and had started giving his older brother shifts at the steakhouse franchise he managed in the north end of the city. It was a pile of time on the TTC, but it was also continuity of time marked on Jared's résumé, and some money to live on. Amy also learned that Jared had played drums in a couple of bands while in university, and that he and his brothers had built a motorcycle from scratch that they tinkered with and rode only when the full consortium was home visiting their folks.

Meanwhile, Jared learned that Amy was not close to her family, nor did she seem all that interested in talking about them. He came to know that she was considering training for a triathlon, and that she had a diverse and strong appreciation of music, while readily acknowledging her own lack of talent in this regard. He particularly enjoyed the moments where she occasionally let her more academic knowledge of what they were observing at the aquarium come through. He loved gaining an inside track on what they were looking at.

"They sense their prey," she said, after they witnessed a strange altercation between a shark and a ray, the ray having surfaced out of invisibility in the sand.

"What do you mean?"

"The hammerhead electromagnetically senses its prey. It feels and knows the ray is there, even though it can't see it. And ray electromagnetically sense its own prey. There is a chain of awareness based on need. Electromagnetics are huge in nature. Their value is way less apparent in our overly developed brains. But it's still there."

Jared spoke of how, once he had managed to get past the commercialism of the aquarium, he had come to enjoy the peace he felt there, and to appreciate how at odds it was with the concrete and capitalist metropolis whose heart it inhabited. He was highly aware of the deliberate re-creation of the aquatic environments. He described feeling cold when he had first noticed the section with all the gauges and meters, the digital displays of such delicately relative numbers; knowing that man's technology was responsible for the life or death, instant or prolonged, of all of these non-human creatures, none of whom were here of their own accord. Amy, on the other hand, had not realized just how much of this aspect of their surroundings she had tuned out.

They walked in silence for some time after that.

"I'm glad I met you," he said on the following week, an unfamiliar statement concluding their familiar period of silence.

There was something wonderfully sincere yet final in his tone. She nodded, her eyes becoming fixated on the thick glass in front of them instead of on the contents beyond. She paused deliberately to create space. She had come to re-acquire some conversational patience through their time together.

"And ... ?" she said, not moving her eyes from the surface of the glass. "I sense an 'and.'"

He touched the sleeve of her upper arm lightly. She made herself look at him. His gaze was no different than it had been, but his tone decidedly was. "You're a really interesting person. And, how you've been with me ... you've helped me so incredibly in learning to see that I'm better than my rather huge mistake."

"You're right about the last part," she said, although she would never be able to separate him from it.

"No. Really." He looked down and breathed in, just as had the first time he had told her his story. He resumed her gaze. "We both need to get out of here, don't you think? Reclaim our lives, be more than who or what we needed to be just in here. Maybe I'm crazy, but I feel like it's time for each of us, in our own way, to let this go.

Don't you? The aquarium part, that is." Without conscious thought, he was already partway turned toward the exit. "I'm serious," he said, his tone gentle. "Why don't we agree to meet here less often? I'd be thrilled to go and do whatever and to get together whenever. Text me whenever you want. You've become a friend I very much wish to keep."

She stepped back slightly, a slow feeling of anxiety and dismay beginning to spread through her. She confronted it with an immense effort to keep it from showing. You're stunned, she thought to herself. You're simple and stunned. On what planet did you remotely imagine that this burrowed relationship would go on forever? "Maybe," she said, smiling at the ground with what she hoped he would interpret as coyness, while its true design was to mask the dishonestly of her next words. "Yeah, fair. Maybe it's time."

"I wish you saw what I saw," he said.

Meanwhile, in that same moment, his words triggered the exact feeling she had experienced when she first noticed him: a real degree of desire for human contact. "Yeah. Maybe," she said. Deliberately, he leaned forward.

"Try it with me," he said, the words emerging from the wonderful warmth of his smile.

She knew how much he wanted her to share his excitement about moving on, but she also knew she was way out of her depth. To preserve her own delicate homeostasis, to keep the numbers on her gauges and meters within their critical parameters, she would have to pretend for now. They headed out for coffee. As they walked up the stairs to street level, Amy kept feeling as though a critical item had fallen out of her purse somewhere behind her and that it would be missing by the time she ran back to get it.

She dreamed that night that she had painted the walls of her apartment a light greenish-blue. The reflections of hundreds of pairs of car headlights moved across the walls like slow ripples on the surface of water. Traffic lights created tides in which schools of cars idled, then rushed by, their sounds crashing in a long wave on the shore of her pillow and rushing up to her ear. She woke with a slow peaceful feeling which was ripped away when she saw the the close opaqueness of the grey ceiling directly above her, and she screamed with panic.

The Marathon

It was 5 a.m. and the best time to live in suburbia. No sounds from neighbours. No having to look at neighbours. No having to talk to neighbours. The houses were stoic, silent structures, minding their own business.

And the light. Mostly suburbanites still found it too dark at this time. But it was a gentle light, efficient, reflecting only off of what it absolutely needed to. Marc McAllister thought this was the sun in its most beautiful form.

As he slowed his run, he once again became aware of the sounds that so fully occupied his senses for the first mile or so: his breathing, the swish of his jacket sleeves, the polite clapping of his trainers on pavement, the beating of his heart in his ears. He started to become aware of his body again. His mind was returning to his earthly life. The present was evolving into the future in his mind: shower, breakfast, dressing, driving, emailing, greeting, soft-selling, talking, talking, math, thinking, talking, talking. Talking.

Suburbia stepped up its game to match the increasing pace of Marc's headspace. Front doors closed and car doors opened. Motors were started. Dogs began to bark. People in pyjamas wandered outside to collect a newspaper or something they otherwise needed.

Marathon on Sunday, he thought. He looked down at his GPS watch. Only five miles today. His training was winding down.

It was Tuesday.

He daydreamed briefly about the cabin he planned to build out on the lake. Small. Minimalist. Quiet. A dock off which one could dive. The sound of his head plunging under the water. The soft, diffuse light below the surface.

Josia was 11 years old, and the girliest girl-child Marc had ever met. Her matching pyjama and slipper-clad self was pouring cereal in the kitchen. This was unusual. Princess had taken to sleeping quite late, causing parental panic five days out of seven as she slept through snooze after snooze, yet somehow managing to get on the bus with zero seconds to spare. Marc and Josia had met following the first date between him and her mother seven years ago. Josia mostly called him Dad at this point. She called him Marc when he didn't say the "right" things.

He didn't quite get kids. Especially ones who talked hair and nail polish and One Direction at a high frequency. Their complicity was based on Josia being exceptionally bright. She saw this part of herself in her stepfather, and they each knew the other could take a challenge. While he didn't understand her most of the time, he had come to adore her, and had more than bought into his part of preparing the best possible future for her.

He stood silently for a moment, watching the unusual event which was the preparation of her own breakfast. She looked up at him and held his gaze briefly. The challenge.

"Soooo," he said, trying not to lean his sweaty self against anything in particular. He gestured across the breakfast setup. "To what do we owe this event? Did you mis-set your alarm? Did the school get its own mall?"

"Ha ha." Josia went straight to the business of eating. He stood patiently. She looked up. "Do you not have a job to go to?"

"Seriously, Josh. I'm really curious."

"Soccer training camp. Did you forget?"

"Did you forget you hate sports?"

She smiled. "I don't hate Jason Lawless. Or road trips. Or getting out of class early for road trips."

"Ah. Les bénéfices secondaires."

"Speak English," she said.

"Pay attention in French class," he shot back with a smile. Or any class, he thought. It was mildly alarming, how quickly things entered and cemented in her mind. It left her a great deal of time to ponder things like Jason Lawless. When would she hit a wall where she finally had to learn what work was? Perhaps Jason Lawless wasn't such a bad idea, if he got her feigning interest in a sport. She would have to go to practice and actually work at something that had not, as of yet, come naturally to her. One could become so terribly trapped by what came naturally.

"Is your mother driving you?"

"Supposed to."

Marc nodded to himself. "I'd better make sure she's up then."

"That'd be great."

More car doors slammed outside as he climbed the stairs. The light, to him, had become more harsh. Less forgiving.

Dawn was mostly awake. She was scrolling through whatever "news" was on her phone, catching up on whatever people had done between 11 p.m. and 7 a.m. Dawn had Fear-of-Missing-Out syndrome.

"Hi," he said, taking off his watch and placing it gently on his dresser.

"Hi."

"So your child has found motivation to rise?"

She laughed. "Yeah. Guess so." She took one last look at something on her phone and rolled around in a failed attempt to get out of bed. "Suppose I should support that effort by getting up."

While the undercurrent of his thoughts had gained a pulsing momentum in anticipation of the day ahead, already overtaking his earlier space and peace of mind, his body still felt tranquil. Calibrated. Plus, he was mildly pleased with Josh's initiative. "I'll take her," he said suddenly.

"Don't you have a meeting right off?" she asked in a slower, sleepier voice, the acceptance of his offer immediate. Like daughter, like mother. They loved their sleep.

Marc shrugged. "I'm sure I can get away with a five minute delay."

He was likely right. He had taken a degree in finance, but was extraordinarily gifted in languages. As an entry-level advisor, at a firm where he had never intended to stay, he turned heads and career direction one day when a senior partner was drowning in misdirected and poorly understood debate with a Czech client. Before he fully realized what he was doing, Marc had heard his own voice reassuring the client, in Czech, about his portfolio and even making suggestions. The client had wheeled to face Marc and launched into a frenzied diatribe of words and gestures. The senior partner, while initially infuriated by the interruption, wisely checked his ego long enough for things to settle. The account grew a set of wings that no one had imagined possible.

"How did we not know of this talent?" the senior asked Marc afterward, handing him a scotch.

"Because you didn't give a fuck," Marc replied in Flemish.

"What?" asked the senior, smiling and fully captivated at this point.

"Because you never asked."

Czech. Flemish. German. Spanish. Italian. Light but developing Arabic. French, the language of his father.

"Chinese?" asked the senior earnestly.

Marc was briefly angered, but the only knowing entity was the scotch, heated from Marc's tightening grip on the glass. He created a smile. "Haven't I done my part today, John? Perhaps this year, even?" He raised his glass as the senior raised his.

There was no looking back. Quiet Marc became a specialist with foreign clientele. They flew from all corners of the world to meet the stylish man and enjoy his refreshingly calm demeanour, with no hint of an English accent in any of the additional languages he spoke. He was handsomely compensated. He had a control his seniors knew they did not. He made a daily, sometimes hourly, decision to not take advantage of this.

His demeanour was calm because the only thing that mattered to him was Josh's fate; this being, above all, her chance not to tow the line. Her chance to deliberately choose her own happiness. And, as of next summer, the construction of his cabin on the lake.

Josia's immediate fate was now in the hands of her stepfather. "Not gonna say no," Dawn murmured in response to Marc's offer. She was sound asleep again before she could hear the shower start up.

Josia seemed pleased at this unusual delivery to school at the hands of her stepfather. She knew he was really good at his job. She knew he was really smart, and good-looking. She had noticed that her friends' moms did their best to not stare at him when they dropped their kids off to visit, and then again when they picked them up. Her teachers had never seen him. Her mother handled all things school. Josia imagined that his schedule didn't permit it.

Despite herself, she became more and more animated as the soccer field came into view. Dozens of kids were getting out of vehicles, collecting their too-big sports bags with the help of their parents, and running awkwardly to meet their new team at the bench.

"There's Ashton and Kayla and we're not in the same class this year so we're stoked to be on the same team," she ranted, glowing.

He grinned. "Well, that's awesome." He scanned the curb ahead. "Where do we deposit you?"

"Right up here," she pointed. "That's Jason Lawless's sister, Lauren. And that's their dad with her, too!"

Marc's eyes narrowed as his view of the Lawless father-daughter combo panned closer. He was faced with an almost imperceptibly distorted mirror of himself. The man stood, smiling, in a tailored suit, with a deliberately careless version of the same hairstyle. He was not quite as fit. He stood with the 11-year-old daughter of his very own. Something was tightening in Marc's stomach. He felt alarm. He didn't know why. His eyes didn't move from the father-daughter pair while Josia scrambled from the car, grabbed her stuff from the back seat, and yelled a quick "bye thanks" before slamming the door shut. She scampered away to join the other father and daughter.

The grounded peace of Marc's run in the delicate 5 a.m. light was gone. There was an unpleasant, edgy vibration filling his torso. It was a familiar sensation to him; baseline. But its particular hour was way too early.

A friendly, excited exchange occurred between the two girls. Pleasant and perhaps encouraging words were exchanged with the father. Marc only heard muffled voices; the car windows were closed on account of the air conditioning. The two girls turned to walk toward their team. Marc's eyes never left the man, whose own eyes then roved the girls up and down, and a detached look of fantasy fell across his face. A moment never meant to be observed. A moment reserved for a lap dance. For a hooker.

Marc was out of the car and on top of the man within seconds. The man's facial expression snapped to a look of shock for an instant before the back of his head hit the ground and his face was smashed repeatedly with a fist. Never never never never was the only thought carving circles in Marc's head. Then nothing was in his head.

He slowly became aware of the familiar: his breathing; the beating of his heart in his ears; the sweat running down his face, down his back. He felt himself standing upright. Voices were shouting. A girl was crying.

Marc raised his forearm and looked down at his bloody wrist. There was no watch; no measure of how far he had gone. He would not run the marathon on Sunday. And it no longer mattered.

Sketchfest

Johnston's microbrew pub held an artistic event once a month for 24 months. During this period, the third Wednesday night of each month became Sketchfest.

In the public space known as The Gathering, long tables were brought in and set up. Lovely hand-hewn wooden benches were put into place. People came in around 6:30. They could order the Single Malt Sketch or the Blended Sketch, among the other beers on tap. They chatted some amongst themselves. They casually chose their places; stowed their hats or coats or mittens or motorcycle helmets, depending on the season; placed their pencils on the tables; and opened up their sketchbooks.

At 7 p.m., the music was turned off. A brief announcement in a happy hipster voice said:

"Hello, friends. Welcome to Sketchfest here at Johnston's. If you're back for Sketchfest, then you know what to do. If you are new to Sketchfest, here's the thing: we sketch in complete silence for one hour. Bar service will stop during this time. Of course, feel free to use the bathroom if you have to, or leave the building if you have to, and come back if you want to. But until 8 p.m., no words are to be said. Our staff will be observing the quiet as well. Please silence your cell phones during this time so as to grant yourself, as well as the people around you, the full experience of Sketchfest. At the end, by all means, keep your sketches! But if you wish, you can place them in the box provided in the entryway. We're going to put them all together in May of next year to make one giant piece of art that will become part of the décor and history here at Johnston's! Isn't that exciting? We sure think so. And now, there will be a five count ... to Sketchfest."

And so the hour began.

Sketchfest had some hardcore regulars. It became an artistic and lifestyle endurance test of sorts; an unusual challenge among the city's cultural activities. Also, for those who attended all 24 events, there was to be a draw for the prize of a pint a day for a full year with the apt yet boring title of A Year of Beer.

It was reported that one young man attended all but the last session, which he missed on account of severe food poisoning that occurred while on a first date gone horribly awry at the Snow Crab Festival. He quit drafting school immediately following, and reportedly had a terrible time drawing anything at all for the better part of a year, down to a simple map on a Wendy's drive-thru paper bag for some confused travelers who had flagged him down on his bike. Two long-time friends who were finishing up the last years of their bachelor degrees drew nothing but each other at Sketchfest, with the drawings becoming progressively less flattering. They completed all 24 sessions; neither won the attendance prize, and they were barely speaking by the end. A lady in her mid-sixties was deliberate about Sketchfest, which was a completely new activity in her life. She added new techniques each month. She kept on drawing once the event closed, and had her first gallery showing the year she turned 70.

Some days, the room was full. Others, the Johnstons lost business. And they knew it.

With the singular exception of Sketchfest, Bing and Caleb Johnston saw eye-to-eye about everything within their trendy and quite successful business. Their common vision for the brewery, as well as their twin factor, had been a stroke of marketing genius. They weren't good looking boys, but they had enviable beards, excellent wardrobe, and good carpentry skills. The Gathering was a work of art in and of itself. People came, stayed, left, and returned with friends. The brothers had surpassed their own vision of a room that felt spacious and intimate all at the same time. And they loved beer. They loved, loved, loved beer.

Bing had always been the stronger builder, while Caleb had a slight edge in his inventiveness. Sketchfest was Caleb's. Bing attended the first two events, but then made himself scarce on Wednesday evenings until the run was nearly over. At month six, he gently approached his brother with the thought that it didn't really have to go on for another 18 months, did it, really? By then, Caleb wasn't sure why they would bother for that long, either. But he was committed to his project. In his mind's eye, he saw the back wall of the brewing area covered from floor to ceiling with the sketches of Sketchfest. He would arrange them carefully into a larger image; a gestalt representing some element of brewing, or his family's long-established history in the trades, or perhaps an event of local lore. It would be an extraordinary, organic work of art. The idea excited him tremendously. Meanwhile, Bing shrugged. Sales were otherwise fantastic, and the corporate Christmas cash always flowed generously through The Gathering, which had been booked for several years in advance for staff parties as of its first week of operation.

For the first five or six Sketchfests, Caleb couldn't wait until closing, when he and the night's staff would go through the box of sketches. The staff finished their counts, poured themselves some pints, and sat and laughed with their boss at the fruits of labour produced by the Sketchies, who, for the most part, clearly had more success at their day jobs than they had raw artistic talent. The staff sat in awe of the odd drawing that was highly competent or creative. They had a good laugh when they saw themselves in some of the works. One gifted individual had created a series of sketches reflecting a significant investment in themes of tattooesque snakes, decks of cards, and the heads of the Royal family. Caleb was delighted. The creator of these works was a quiet, young-looking man whose ID decidedly confirmed that he was out of high school. This was so unbelievable to staff that, without fail, they asked him for ID at each Sketchfest. He stopped attending abruptly following session six, and was never seen again.

Following session six, which marked both the young man's disbandment and Bing's delicately framed question to his brother, Sketchfest became a matter of routine. Post-work social time for staff no longer involved an amusing review of the evening's sketches. The box lay untouched until Caleb took it up to his office the next morning.

Bing began counting down three months prior to the end of the two-year run. He couldn't wait for it to be over. Caleb felt similarly, yet he was swept up in the hype that grew around the finale. He did local newspaper and radio interviews, and a couple of television appearances. Bing's disdain lessened as attendance picked up suddenly and forcefully for the final two events. There were lineups. On the final evening, prior to the start of what had been such a peaceful and quiet time in The Gathering, an altercation took place among five individuals who felt they should have the one remaining spot. Unplanned publicity ensued instantly from this bizarre bar fight, which took place outside of a microbrew pub among sober adults shortly before 7 p.m. on a Wednesday. Bing shrugged and checked on his test batches for a new summer-themed ale (he was well tired of brewing Single Malt Sketch) while Caleb handled the police, paramedics, and more media. The prerecorded announcement was heard faintly outside amongst the chaos, and the last event began.

The last event ended. In contrast to the silence, which had been so devoutly honoured for 24 consecutive sessions, attendees and staff alike whooped and hollered as the final five-count signaling the end of Sketchfest played over the PA system. Staff yelled into microphones as they drew the winner of A Year of Beer. This turned out to be an accountant who had attended all 24 events on a bet of $24 with his mother. The music resumed much louder than usual, and The Gathering was packed until closing, for which the police had decided to return. They sat quietly in their cars with nothing to do as everyone left slowly, politely, and legally. They flashed the lights of their cruisers in acknowledgement as they drove away.

Perhaps the full complement of staff was as done with Sketchfest as Bing had been since Month Two. Once the last patrons had left, the doors were locked, pints were pulled, and the staff laughed and chatted until first light about the bar fight and the night's excellent sales. No one thought to empty the sketch box. No one thought to look at anything that had been drawn for the past eighteen months.

The next day, Caleb arrived to work a bit later and more bleary-eyed than usual. Despite his love of beer, he wasn't that much of a drinker. He had surfed the high of the previous evening on a few extra Single Malt Sketch. Bing, on the other hand, looked no different after ten pints than after two. He was inside the glassed-off room within the brewing area that contained his two test tanks. He was holding up two glasses of ale and comparing their colours under extremely bright lights. The extremely bright lights pierced every inch of Caleb's face as he shuffled by on his way up to the office.

Over three trips, Caleb hauled the sketches down to the brewing space, and began to spread them out over the floor. The haze in his head exchanged itself for a growing excitement within his chest as he realized the works would almost exactly cover the 40-by-30-feet wall. He grabbed a ladder from the utility room and almost knocked it over while scrambling up to get a better view of what he might be looking at for an image. Suddenly, he saw an unexpected style among the mass of drawings. He descended and pulled out 24 sketches that were identical in their style and quality of shading. On a separate space of the floor, he arranged and re-arranged them until he saw what he thought had been intended. Someone had beaten him to the gestalt. He went over to the glass wall and knocked to get his brother's attention.

The two stood and looked down at the set of twenty-four drawings. Like the wooden walls of The Gathering, the images mostly resembled the ringed interior of large logs, the delicate shading on the paper delineating the lines and grain that told the age of the wood. Within each drawing, a single word emerged almost imperceptibly from the grain. The twenty-four words, as arranged by Caleb, spelled out:

eight years gone by I am married now my heart still aches on cold nights when the stars are shining out over our lake

Caleb looked to his brother, and then back to the drawings. He tried to imagine who the author and artist might have been; which individual had sat there once a month for two full years and crafted this deliberate message. Was the artist male or female. What did he / she look like. Caleb was stunned. How had he lost track of the detail he absorbed so excitedly in The Gathering over the first few events? He had studied their faces, their postures, their choice of drinks, their calm and their restlessness as it ebbed and flowed over the hour of silence. How had the extraordinary condensed so imperceptibly into routine?

Caleb's head swam in a mix of astonishment, curiosity, and hangover. He shifted back and forth, and wondered why his brother still hadn't said anything. Just as Caleb opened his mouth to speak, Bing shrugged and handed him one of the glasses of ale he still held in his hands, steering Caleb's eyes away from the redness of his own face.

Ike-o

Every Wednesday evening, Ike sat in his maroon-red Ford Focus in the parking lot outside the Birchwood Motor Lodge and Restaurant and listened to Peter, Paul, and Mary. He had been doing this for four years. A staff member finally remarked the pattern outside and alerted the Birchwood's manager, Danny.

"Make no mind," said Danny. "It's Ike."

Ike had lost his wife suddenly to causes never confirmed. On a Wednesday night, they had gone out to supper at the Birchwood, newly acquired by his distant cousin Danny. Ike and his wife returned home. They put away an extra Coors Light or two (it was date night, after all) and Ike woke up next to a stiff and unbreathing Theresa. Ike was 74. Theresa had been 63.

Over hundreds of Wednesdays, Ike never cracked a window in the Ford. He never entered the building.

The building was a rustic log structure, the décor of which had been frozen in time long before Danny had taken it over. Leather padded doors. Giant, long-silent pay phones. Taxidermied game heads. The moose, while magnificent, lasted only a month on account of flaking apart and garnishing Bill Norton's chicken

43

wings. Danny's brand new business would have tanked instantly had the moose's remains chosen to adorn anyone else's plate. Bill was a career woodsman who loved to tell tales, real or not, of eating anything he could kill with his bare hands. "Been so long since I had moose!" Bill had hollered at the rest of the lounge. He actually lifted a wing to his mouth just as Danny appeared like wildfire, swiping the plate with one hand and the wing with the other.

"We outta make posters," Sophie, a pretty, nose-pierced young server said one Wednesday night to Brianna, her nose-pierced server best friend. "DJ Ike / Every Wed Nite / Party in the Parkin Lot! Weee-ooo!" They broke into laughter and high-fived.

"Say again?" said Danny, behind them. The two straightened up, went pale, and bolted for the dining room to check needlessly on their customers.

"Not yet," Mitch said repeatedly the following evening, during a weekly photography class.

"Baaaah!" puffed Danny. It was Sunset Photography Week. "Why??"

"Colours aren't right yet," said Mitch with exaggerated calm, smiling at Danny's impulsivity. "They'll get stronger. Wait."

"They're pretty now!" insisted Danny.

"Wait."

Mitch was right. Danny hated when Mitch was right, especially when he nailed a shot and saw Mitch's sermon of patience confirmed in frame.

The field trip concluded and the students dispersed. Mitch meandered over to Danny, his friend since eighth grade. He had gotten his shot, but had not remotely recovered from the effort of stillness.

"Geez that was hard!" Danny exclaimed, launching his backpack into the backseat of his Jeep.

"So is Ike still doing that thing outside the restaurant every Wednesday?" Mitch asked.

"Yeah. Why?" Danny was now puzzled as well as huffy.

Mitch shrugged. "Doncha think it's weird?"

"Doncha think it's weird?" Danny mimicked in a high-pitched voice. Mitch rolled his eyes in attempt to mask the scathing condescendence that he felt. "I am giving my widower cousin the space to grieve," Danny continued. "People do unusual things when they grieve. What is so wrong with letting a harmless guy do an unusual but harmless thing?"

"Is it all that harmless?" asked Mitch, with an edge that rang with Danny.

"What?" Danny asked, now all business.

Mitch paused. "People talk, Danny. You're not the only game open year-round here anymore. Dontcha you think people might want to go eat where the weird grieving guy ain't?"

Danny planted. "They can go, then," he said evenly.

"No worries," said Mitch. His words and tone were sincere, the truce achieved. It was not their first. "Just thought you should know. No one will tell you but me."

Danny nodded. They got into their respective cars. Danny couldn't say thanks, but it was understood.

Danny himself had never married, or really even come close. His sense of adventure resided in a single trip to Europe in his 20s, which had resulted in the cultivation of a decent culinary palate. Years later, this experience was incorporated unobtrusively into the dining experience of the Birchwood. Danny was otherwise known for his attention to detail, dry sense of humour, and quick temper. He dressed well enough, but refused to engage in activities favourable to physical fitness. In a small town, he wasn't an easy match.

In a small town, Danny felt terribly for his distant cousin Ike.

The pattern of Wednesdays and the other Ikeless days rolled through November into the overcast cold of December. By contrast, the interior climate of the town's favourite restaurant was bright and exciting for staff and patrons alike.

Christmas Eve fell on a Wednesday that year.

It was always a predictably busy day until 3 p.m.: this was the magic hour where avoiders and drinkers felt the need to oblige their loved ones, or otherwise leave everyone else to oblige their own. Danny had been externally smiling and internally cringing all day. What the hell was he going to do with Ike? It was the fifth anniversary of Christmas without his wife. I'd bring a hose that day, thought Danny dramatically, his eyes narrowing as he looked outside where the habitual parking spot lay in morbid but loving waiting.

He was tallying receipts when Sophie and Brianna approached him. "Yeah, we have an idea," Sophie said, pursuing a conversation that had started in her head but not in reality.

Danny had little time for the pair since Sophie had pulled the DJ Ike joke, but he sat quietly as they presented a crushed receipt, pointed to the kitchen where Smoke Break Jeremy paced, and then looked to Danny for what would be his approval or their notice. He nodded wordlessly.

The restaurant sat dark as the impeccably polished Ford crunched through a light snowfall at 5:44 p.m. The muted folk music began at 5:45 p.m. The restaurant lights went back on. Jeremy, Brianna, Sophie, and Danny carried the exact meal that Ike and Theresa had shared on their last evening together out to the car on two separate trays.

Ike's white, scruffy face stared out through his glasses at the four winter coats and two trays, bewildered. The windows scrolled down on both sides. They passed the trays in. The music gained a fullness that no one outside the car had ever heard. Sophie burst into tears, as did Jeremy; Danny and Brianna finished a steady delivery on their own. The car windows scrolled up.

Back inside the restaurant, Danny poured his staff a hefty gin and tonic. He congratulated them on their reconnaissance mission of kindness. He wondered silently at their simple idea, which had somehow never crossed what he had always considered to be his own relatively intelligent mind.

The following Wednesday, Danny didn't think twice as he sent the staff home early on New Year's Eve. He shut off all the lights and was about to head out as headlights swung across the front windows.

Stop it, he thought, panicked and fully terrified. Five years. New Year's Eve. The guy could totally set up to gas himself right here. Jesus Christ. This can't be happening. Danny hyperventilated himself into putting on his toque and gloves and stomping around in circles, priming for some sort of action with no idea of what that could possibly be.

Wait, he thought.

He moved himself slowly along the wall toward the back of the restaurant. He could see Ike's profile in the car, cast by the security light. He sat down at the edge of a wooden chair, clutching his phone in his gloved hand until Ike drove away punctually at 7 p.m. Danny despairingly yet thankfully called Mitch instead of 911.

"Guess yer Last Supper idea didden work," said Mitch, with the best consoling tone he could muster, four drinks in. "Come over here, we're just gettin starded."

Four drinks later himself, Danny too was just gettin starded. It was a great night. He awoke with a start shortly after 1 p.m., finding himself semi-tucked in on a sofa with a bucket beside him. He wandered from what he recognized as Mitch's den into a brightly lit kitchen and saw, by the déjà vu of the clothing on various adults around the room, that he had not been the only passer-outer. "Happy New Year?" he asked, slowly. Everyone laughed.

Within days, the world went back to normal operations. Danny was relieved. He found himself anticipating another level of relief when he imagined that Ike, finally freed from grief, would not show up that week. Danny's hopes were fully dashed when Smoke Break Jeremy returned from a smoke break with the news of Ike's arrival.

"Ohhhh no," said Danny. He had been wanting so badly to release his distant cousin from a terrible torment. The meal had been a fail. The New Year had been a fail.

What do I do, thought Danny. I want to help you. How do I help you?

A few locals sat in the lounge, drinking draft beneath the large, badge-shaped outline that marked the legend of Bill Norton and the flaking taxidermied moose head. Danny shook his own head, poured himself a draft, and uncharacteristically sat down to chat. This was something he usually reserved for the morning coffee crowd. Two draft and a pile of half-bizarre, mostly hilarious stories later, generally about which Hargrove was in jail these days, Danny's head was full of scenarios other than Ike's. He headed home.

The following Wednesday came and went without Ike.

The entire staff took notice shortly after 6 p.m. The parking spot was empty. Each set of tires and headlights belonged to a car other than Ike's.

Danny commanded the end of the night with calm. "Great night, guys, thank you," he said, waving them away.

"But –" started Brianna.

"G'night," Danny declared, not looking up from his receipts.

Then he sat. Alone. And, yet again, frightened. He called Mitch.

"Wait," said Mitch.

"Baaaaah!" raged Danny, and hung up.

He waited for two Ikeless weeks. At the end of January, he called his Aunt Myrna.

"Oh. Danny!" she yelled joyously into the phone. His older, deaf aunt refused to wear hearing aids, or otherwise listen well, and the screeching quality of her voice made Danny's head ring.

Danny learned three compellingly yelled facts: that Ike had met some lady across the border; that Ike was happy as a clam; that Danny himself needed more.

He trained Brianna as an assistant manager.

He created a dating profile for himself on www.pro-cupid.net.

"What the hell?" asked Mitch, looking at a dating profile featuring his own photo portrait of his friend, which was quite nice considering the significant challenge it had posed for both photographer and subject. "I thought I was doing that for your Chamber of Commerce profile."

"Screw that. I'm way overdue for an adventure, wouldn't you say?" smiled Danny, clearly entertained by Mitch's reaction.

Danny's profile handle, Ike-o_75, had 45 new messages.

Intermission

The light in the kitchen darkened slowly around the couple, increasing the pallor of their skin under a single lamp that swung almost imperceptibly a few feet above them. The woman sat sideways to the table, one arm against its edge while the other sat in her lap, her hand closed in a veiny fist. She appeared to be experiencing both anger and anxiety.

The man slowly walked around the table, his breathing loud and his steps deliberate. Finally, he stood almost directly behind the woman. He placed his hands on the table in front of him and leaned the profile of his face into hers. "You owe me," he said, a sound of metered anger and deep betrayal. "But first, you owe me one hell of an explanation."

Then all of the light went from the kitchen.

A beat, and restrained applause began. It gathered polite momentum.

One hundred and eighty degrees from the proscenium, the applause diminished as the house lights came up, revealing a theatre that was about 3/4 full of generally white middle-class individuals, stretching and slowly extricating themselves from blue velvet seats. They began to trickle out the side door leading to the lobby.

"You coming?" Ellie asked Michael.

Michael blinked behind his trendy but thick glasses and slowly rose. His wife had already turned to her friend Alysia and Alysia's husband, Rob. At six feet four inches tall, black, and built like a model, Rob was the visual anomaly of the crowd's demographic composition. A show unto himself, he inevitably invited staring by the virtues of his God-given contrast and beauty. Rob, Alysia, and Ellie chatted their way out the door while Michael followed a few steps back, hands in his pockets, surrounded by people talking about the play. The herd bloomed down the hallway and parted between the bar and the washrooms.

Rob turned from the bar and handed Michael a glass of rye and ginger. "It's a double," he smiled. "Helpful?"

"Hoping so," replied Michael.

Looking around at crowd, and then turning back to Michael, Rob asked, "What is it you hate so much about this, anyway?"

"Intermission."

Rob giggled with his mouth full of wine and swallowed quickly to prevent choking. "What? Come on."

"No." Michael shook his head emphatically. He stepped forward and pointed at the bar. "Look at this," he said. "Intermission is to make money. That's it. It's selfish. We don't need a break. The play didn't need a break. I doubt the actors needed it; there are six of them, and only two on stage at a time. How can they possibly be tired?" His torso rotated slightly, his arms spread out just above waist level. "They're also trying to sell the art on these walls. More money. And the box office – " he continued to point and gesture – "is making money off a pre-sale for something. We sheep are shelling out all this extra money when we've already spent a pile of it on a play that didn't need interruption. On a whole section my life that didn't need interruption." His left arm collapsed to his side and he raised his drink with the other. He paused, looking to Rob in a dual state of resignation and preparation for rebuttal.

Ellie stepped in with her Cheshire Cat grin and a hint of a glare directed at her husband. "I've always enjoyed how committed he is to his opinions," she said dryly. She took Rob by his athletic arm under his always impeccable shirt. "Let's go comfort Alysia. She feels the play will end badly. And let Cranky McCrankerson here stew in his own hatred of nothing in particular."

Michael welcomed this, fully aware that she was only trying to give him some space. He nodded and found himself following his feet over to one of the larger canvases on the wall. Just before he reached a comfortable viewing distance, a younger couple dressed in bleached denim punk attire, adorned with the necessary band patches and chains and wearing tall black boots, crossed rapidly in front of him. They held hands and giggled as they made a beeline for the door, radiant with the confidence of people who don't look back. Comps, he thought. Someone gave them tickets. For free. They can leave now, yet still say they went. He wished he was them.

Looking slowly back to the bar, Michael remarked a lull in service. The two female bartenders were checking their phones. They did not interact. In fact, he perceived a distinct tension emanating from their posture. Wow. They totally hate each other, he thought. Patrons approached the bar; the two millennials burst into practiced smiles and advanced. Time to make money. Michael snorted to himself. Always the money.

Behind him, a reporter of sorts began interviewing someone who was clearly an actor of some repute, although it seemed by their conversation that the actor's work was not at all recent. How can this interview possibly be interesting, thought Michael. The voices of the interviewer and interviewee were equally crafted in their content and light dusting of sincerity. As the crowd became aware of the presence of both actor and media, it started to gather around them. Michael stepped away from the compressed cluster of people and in toward the canvas.

There was a lot of colour, applied in a seemingly random way, over old photographic images of horses tied to trees. Looking closely, he saw that the texture of the horses' bodies had been carefully and subtly altered to consist of anatomically correct hearts. He blinked several times through his thick glasses. Suddenly, he found himself tensing up as though someone was standing too close behind him. He jumped sideways when he realized this was actually happening.

"Like the play?" asked the older, well-groomed gentleman. He wore a nice cardigan and had a spark to his gaze.

"Dunno," replied Michael, nonplussed.

"It's shit," said the man. "Just say it. Say it out loud. It's as brown as the sky is blue."

Michael nodded to himself. "I do hate it. I hate intermission way more, though. It's prolonging the agony."

"Why are you here? Wife?"

"Yes. I very much prefer watching golf."

"Wanna smoke a joint?"

It was Michael's turn to choke on his drink. "No, thanks," he replied, recovering quickly. "Not my thing." What the hell? he though to himself. What kind of vibe am I giving off here?

The man shrugged and carried off into the crowd. Michael turned back to the canvas and then decided to not bother figuring it out anymore. He made his way to the washroom.

To his relief, the washroom contained no one. He finished his business and headed toward the door, feeling almost ready to endure the remainder of the play. He opened the door and found himself faced squarely with the biggest ghost of his past.

The ghost bore a look of shock, as if she too had seen one. She collected herself quickly, but deliberately refused eye contact.

You're still beautiful, was Michael's only and involuntary thought. "Excuse me," the ghost said in a low voice to no one in particular as she shuffled backward, brushing against a few different people and apologizing on her way to the nearest exit. In her rush to get away from Michael, she left the exit door swinging wide open into the poorly lit back alley. Inside, the lights began to blink, signaling the end of intermission.

Michael himself blinked a few more times under his glasses. He lifted the frames off his face and pressed his fingers and thumb to his eyes. His heart slammed against his chest. Five years? Five years. Five years since he had last seen her, without her knowing, at the home show. She has been standing with a little boy who blinked repeatedly behind his own thick glasses, who Michael realized was very likely his son. Their son. Since that day at the home show, he had decided to let sleeping dogs lie. Except this sleeping dog was laughing and growing and probably playing video games and learning how to spell new words, including a last name that wasn't Michael's.

Ellie was the one to spell Michael's last name, having taken it as her own at their wedding just one month prior to the run-in at the home show. Ellie, who had just learned that she couldn't conceive.

The lights blinked again. Michael made a beeline for his seat. He was there before the others.

"You made it through intermission?" asked Rob teasingly, settling back into the blue velvet chair. Alysia and Ellie were deep in gossipy conversation about a couple sitting two rows ahead.

"Guess I did," said Michael, producing what he hoped was a passable smile. He turned his gaze and thoughts to the proscenium ahead and waited, with unbearable impatience, for the mediocre fictional drama to offset the real-life discomfort of his own.

Le Secret professionnel

The Bay Channel Hospital dropped the 'Psychiatric' moniker from its title in 1985. This didn't affect much, except perhaps the perception of the few tourists passing through who happened to notice the building.

Tourists always passed through, as there was little for them to do in the Bay Channel area. Options for activities consisted of an elite fishing and hunting camp about 40 kilometres south of the hospital; and a small, poorly lit Museum of Refrigeration Technology, which fronted a manufacturing plant for industrial kitchen refrigeration equipment.

Built in 1894, the Bay Channel Hospital was a surprisingly friendly and lovely marriage of contemporary rock-steel-window design, with the lower and upper walls of the original structure left standing proudly through. Most areas of the facility had been entirely done over in the early 2000s, and were still quite fresh-looking. Meanwhile, some of the building's back corridors, storage areas, and seldom-used common rooms hadn't seen much reno action since the late 70s. Staff behaved in a polarized way about these zones. They traversed them either in casual oblivion, or in a brisk trot powered by a hair-raising case of the creeps.

Within the hospital's walls, the last two rounds of administration had done much to revamp the hospital's culture, with outstanding results. The BCH attracted highly competent and caring workers, and psychiatry residents from all corners of the country. Other university students from business and social science domains alike had conducted and published research on the resident–staff interaction.

Andrew, known commonly as Drew, usually had no qualms about going to work. He had been at the hospital for nearly five years now, hired immediately following the practical hours of his Resident Care Worker program, which had followed his Bachelor of Social Work. Almost everyone he encountered personally and professionally raised an eyebrow at his order of operations. "I didn't really love systems or community program work," he replied consistently. The questioning rolled off him now; it didn't at first. He didn't want to say how much he had pushed through his degree simply to finish it. It amounted to four long and largely uninteresting years for him. He had never really wanted to go to university.

Among the BCH staff, Drew's education was respected and appreciated. All of his letters were on his ID. It provided fodder for discussion with new and more coherent residents. It provided a stronger salary than would be expected, although not that of a registered social worker.

His girlfriend questioned his career path only once, a year ago, approximately two years into their relationship. He was calm in explaining his choices. She saw his conflict, heard his compassion, and expressed how terrible she felt about what had very much come across as calling him down. She never mentioned it again. She had just finished her law degree. They wouldn't be worried about money.

Drew was also a supervisor on evening and night shifts on the men's C Unit, which was occupied by individuals of little cognizance, a few of whom were still quite physically capable. This wasn't his preferred line of work at the hospital. What he enjoyed most was getting to know the residents, and figuring out what worked for each one of them in terms of helping them cope even the tiniest bit better. He participated willingly with the psychology staff in delivering various individual and group programs. The residents took to him easily. A young man in his late 20s, relatively close in age to Drew, responded particularly well to Drew's presence.

Nathan, known most frequently as Nate, was by far the youngest resident, and also in possession of the greatest degree of functioning. There were others of his age and younger, but they were far less visible within the hospital due to more profound or deteriorating conditions. Drew had seen residents from the advanced care levels only a handful of times, if at all. Both he and his supervisors agreed that Drew's skills were best applied with residents who functioned within relatively moderate levels of impairment. There was no one living at the facility whose wounds, states, or disorders could be considered mild.

Nate's personal history was tragic, although even the "happier" stories among the residents' pre-hospitalization biographies were rarely any degree of pretty. Nate had been severely abused as a child by his father and uncle, resulting in head trauma from which there was never enough time to recover prior to the next blow. This was worsened by injuries incurred during attempts to play hockey and football, which represented Nate's best efforts to fit in while in school. Finally, a misdirected dive off of a cliff into the wrong section of a swimming hole set in motion the terrible but clear path that would bring him to Bay Channel. Mood swings. Emotional outbursts at unemotional times. Unprovoked and explosive physical altercations, often with males older than himself. Unprovoked and explosive physical altercations with women he dated briefly, which numbered many. He was a good-looking young man, as well as funny and charming when not overstimulated. Then came the court appearances. Then the destruction of his own apartment with his bare hands. Another court appearance. The destruction of two rooms in two consecutive rooming houses. And, finally, the death of what was to be his final landlord, three days following an unfortunate decision on the landlord's part to step between Nate and whatever Nate saw behind the walls.

In his newest home, Nate still sometimes snapped. At first he had snapped a lot, and staff response was called accordingly. Time for adjustment, a job helping the older female residents get seated at supper and then helping them back to their wing afterward, and the reward of playing pool with his favourite staff had helped Nate to settle in. Many of the older ladies became smitten, and therefore agitated on the days when the charming young man was in the one-to-one care unit on account of safety concerns, which, unbeknownst to them, rendered him not remotely charming.

Nate eventually settled in far better than anyone had ever expected. He tended to relax by another small degree when Drew was around. For reasons no one understood, and which Drew tried to not make about himself, the sound of Drew's voice was highly calming to Nate. Sometimes, during Nate's meltdowns, it was simply too late. But often, if Drew spoke to him before the critical point, everyone was spared the code call.

Drew did not overtly show favouritism toward Nate. But the positive connection between the two was authentic and apparent. On one particular evening shift, resident and worker were decorating the cafeteria for the October birthday celebrations. They performed victory dances, cheers, and high-fives after each colourful strip of ribbon was twisted and taped into place. The very rare sound of Nate's laughter never went unnoticed.

"Hard not to get attached, eh?" said Bonnie on the next evening's shift. She and Drew stood around in the staff lounge, taking their turns heating up meals in the microwave.

The comment was out of the blue, and Drew wondered where it was coming from. "Suppose. I don't really think about it."

Bonnie watched her supper as it bubbled and carouseled behind the glass. "Maybe you should."

He laughed. "Why?"

Bonnie stood quite a bit taller than most people, which was easily a good six inches taller than Drew. The height of her grey hair in its perpetual bun didn't add any subtlety. She was a fridge of a woman. The Nurse Ratchett references were not lost on her, even though they were only rarely said aloud. Within a few seconds of being in her presence, it was clear that Bonnie commanded gentleness above all else. She also commanded years of experience, assertiveness, knowledge, training, and re-training. She would retire sooner than later. The occasion was already spoken of with sadness. Drew wasn't alone in thinking a lot of her.

Bonnie also commanded a self-appointed mentor role, and engaged in what the staff affectionately referred to as Mentor Moments. These were offered far more than they were solicited. Her input was welcomed the vast majority of the time. At this particular time, however, Drew was not feeling terribly open to a Mentor Moment. His stomach growled audibly and he felt a mild sadness at not having arrived at the microwave first.

"We have to find a place where they don't go," she said. "That no matter how much a patient makes you laugh, or does well because of you, or kicks you in the groin or pulls your hair or drools on you or spits at you or calls you the names of demons you've never even heard of, they hit a wall in your heart, and dissolve before they can reach who you are. And who you are to those closest to you."

The microwave beeped, and Bonnie removed her Rubbermaid container. Drew stood for a second before he looked to his own container on the counter, and then set it on the carousel.

"Ok," he said hesitantly, pressing some buttons and watching the nuclear ride start up again. "But honestly, I've never worried about it. It sucks when you lose people, but I've been OK about that so far. I'm not sure what you're getting at, I guess."

Bonnie plunked her spoon into her container and faced Drew. "You're good at what you do," she said, with a warm smile, "but not immune. Inoculate yourself. Tend to your head sometime, like you tend to that immaculate beard of yours. Check in. Check out. Maintain instead of having to fix something later."

"What is with the speech?" Drew laughed, now annoyed, yet trying to keep things light. "Did you set your retirement date? Do I look sad? What?"

"You're a good guy. Just don't wait," she said. Her giant right hand carried her supper ahead of her as she gave him a friendly pat on the back with her giant left hand. The third code of the shift was called on the men's C Unit. They paused to listen to the call. Bonnie, who was the primary C Unit supervisor that night, carried on with a bit of speed. "Storm en route," she said cheerily behind her.

Storm en route. Sad but true, Drew thought at he sat on the couch and started shovelling leftover steak and rice into his hungry mouth. He was not on call for codes this evening. He was more than OK with that. He started planning his weekend, the food began to work its magic, and the confusing traces of Bonnie's words faded into the pleasing yet uninspiring décor of the lounge.

The following evening, at the beginning of the next shift, Drew found Nate reading while in front of the TV. "A Game of Thrones," said Drew, sounding impressed. "What made you pick this one?"

Nate stretched out his short but solid frame, and set the book onto the nearest table. "Ahhh I dunno," he drawled. "Coach said it was a good place to start from where I left off." His head moved slowly, and his eyes set focus on the TV.

"How was the lightning storm last night?" asked Drew. "I heard it was massive. I slept through the whole thing though."

"Heard some bells and voices and stuff," said Nate, his blue eyes and blonde scruff still facing the moving images of the television. His face was unusually impassive. "The storm didn't wake me up or keep me up."

"Good, good," replied Drew.

It was one of those days where it was taking his charge a little longer than usual to come around. Drew paused and sat down in the institutionally upholstered chair diagonal to Nate. He let some time pass as they both looked at but did not really watch TV. There were two other residents gathered in the TV area, one male and one female, both much older. The male resident was clean shaven, but in terrible need of a haircut on his few remaining bolts of white hair. He wore all denim, his clothing hanging in the way that clothing hangs when you do not dress yourself. The female resident stared at the TV with a meaningful gaze for periods of time, interspersed with other periods of watching what seemed to be an invisible tennis match on the ceiling. Periodically, she smiled.

"Something on your mind?" Drew finally and gently asked Nate.

Nate shrugged again, and was quiet for a while. Then he asked, "How old will I be when I get out?"

Get out? thought Drew. He then chose a different direction for his response. "Well, how long have you been here?"

"Not long, as far as I can tell." Nate shook his head. "I don't remember a lot of the beginning parts."

"Hardly anyone one does." Drew's reply was calm and honest. "It's a big change for a lot of people." He paused again, then asked, "Is this something you've been thinking of more lately?"

"TV might not be good for me. Been trying to read." Nate had learned forward and clasped his hands. Drew could see the energy and motion transferring slowly from hand to hand, veins rising and falling. "Been trying to read."

Drew delicately rose to his feet, briefly touching Nate on the elbow at the same time. "Read later when you don't have someone to shoot hoops with." He leaned his head toward the courtyard. A well-appointed basketball court and garden area lay beyond the shatterproof glass windows. Plastic picnic tables in their bright colours and even brighter reflections in the large puddles left over from the rainfall delineated the perimeter of the common area. The extra burst of colour provided a stunning distraction from the dual-layer razor wire fence that stood 40 feet beyond the court, and from the eyes of the surveillance cameras that saw every corner of the facility and its grounds. "Real air, Nate. How about it?"

Nate had risen without thinking, more because of the quick touch than the verbal suggestion. "Hoops?" he asked, as though it had been his idea.

"We're on," replied Drew. Was it the storm? he asked himself.

Hoops went fine. The rest of the shift went fine. Nate said, "See ya tomorrow," with a smile, and Drew went home. Drew didn't reconsider the circumstances until the next evening, after he had finished his shower and was getting dressed for a night shift as primary supervisor on C Unit.

He came out to grab his lunch bag and to say goodnight to his girlfriend, who was hanging out on the couch in yoga pants with her iPad and a glass of wine. It was a Friday night, and it marked the end of her articling at a firm that was intent on hiring her. "This looks fun," he said, wishing for the first time in a long time that he could stay and play with her in their light, easy, safe, way at home.

She smiled as he hugged her from behind and kissed her cheek. She took another draw of wine. The liquid in the glass glowed a beautiful, deep red in the dimmed light of their apartment, with fresh fall air coming in slow waves through the open balcony doors. "Get home and try to slip in without waking me," she said. "We'll pretend we went to bed together and then slept in or something."

He smiled. "Deal," he said. It was really hard to leave her tonight. He didn't know why.

Past the check-in point, Drew was met by Bonnie; Jolene, the psychologist; and Dr. Grigor, the psychiatrist on duty that evening. "Shift change brief," said Bonnie. This occurrence was not unusual, nor was the configuration of people. Drew couldn't read Bonnie, though, which puzzled him.

The oddly shaped group of individuals marched down the corridor. Giant Bonnie, in her off-white scrubs, was nearly twice the size of the petite psychologist, who didn't understand what it was to dress down for work in a psychiatric institution. Dr. Grigor was short and round, and looked much older than he was. The variety of people connected by means of a workplace was sometimes staggering to Drew. This was more apparent to him tonight, perhaps because of or despite the lack of apparent concern from the others as they walked along the hall. Drew himself had begun to feel nothing but.

They sat down in the principal conference room. Dr. Grigor began the briefing. "Nathan Blakeney incurred a traumatic brain injury last night at approximately 9:50 p.m. It was nothing deliberate or foreseen. He seems to have slipped in the shower, hit his head, and lost consciousness. Given his history of head trauma and volatile behaviour, he remains in Medical for the moment. Results of the MRI just reached us about an hour ago." Dr. Grigor, an avoidant yet compassionate man, was now speaking directly to Drew. "It is expected that we will not see the same young man we met initially," he said. "Another level of care will be required. Fine motor functioning is and may remain somewhat compromised. Speech production will be altered, and short term memory likely all but eradicated. Impulse control will undoubtedly be more impaired. We can't take chances regarding his safety and the safety of those around him at this time. He'll be moved to C Unit in a day or two."

Drew took in the information, placing his shield of training and education before him. "So he'll be on my shift there as of this weekend," said Drew, looking to Dr. Grigor, who nodded.

"Yes," he said, "although we are putting in extra staff for a while. There isn't as much time for acclimatization as we would like, but we also don't feel it wise to send him to IPI just yet."

"Good," said Drew, maintaining a calm voice and deliberate eye contact with the others at the table. The Intensive Psychiatric Intervention unit housed those of the most profound levels of impairment. 'Intervention' was a reframe and a misnomer. IPI was the end of the line.

"Good, yes. I agree," said Dr. Grigor, "but there will still be some rough sailing. We will see how he does. This is no less of a transition than when he first came to us. We all need to remember that. Any questions?" He raised his inflection toward the rest of the table without looking up from a note he was making in a chart.

"No. Thank you," they said individually. Dr. Grigor excused himself, and the remainder followed. Jolene and her petite permasmile headed for the checkpoint exit. She had stayed late for the briefing. It occurred to Drew that Bonnie was on his shift for the next three days. He felt comforted and suddenly resentful all at the same time. Had she seen this coming, somehow?

For several minutes, the two walked silently toward C Unit. "Sad news," offered Bonnie, finally.

Drew nodded, not looking up. "Yeah. Super sad." He didn't want to betray how awful he felt. Poor Nate had no way to win, ever, faced with the conditions of his existence. But now it was as though the walls of the most stable time he had ever known in life had suddenly fallen in, leaving him, in a sense, buried alive. Drew got control over his own breathing, which he hadn't realized he'd lost. "Any word on how he's feeling? Does he realize what's happened?"

"Groggy and slow, for now. He thinks he fell and hit his head, that's all," replied Bonnie. "They haven't told him he's moving yet, though. That's tomorrow."

Nothing further was said. Drew was grateful. The shift came and went. In its quieter moments, Drew scanned the unit and its high, narrow windows, and its open beds with the short, padded dividers between them. He had great trouble imagining Nate in one of the beds alongside the older men who drooled or howled or both, or were seated at the table under a cheerful cardboard calendar with slots marking periods of time such as Day / Month / Year / Season. Fall, it read tonight. Fall, Nathan did. Drew eventually went home to slide into bed with his girlfriend, who said nothing as he held her a little tighter than usual before he fell asleep.

Drew continued to have no difficulty sleeping as the weeks went on. Nate, however, slept only when highly sedated. His introduction to C Unit had, as expected, been intensely challenging. The quick temper was back in force, and the frequency and severity of his mood swings had increased. He was clearly frustrated at not being able to put words together as he could before. For the first few weeks, Nate could not recall being told that he was now living on C Unit. As a result, the situation was entirely new to him hour to hour. He spent quite a bit of time in a separate care area with one-to-one staffing. Eventually this became more unpleasant to him than the ongoing surprise of his move to C Unit. His levels of aggression toward staff and other residents decreased enough for him to remain on C Unit, albeit under a fair degree of chemical restraint.

Interaction with residents on C Unit was generally one-sided, whether it originated from resident or staff. Patterns of communication with Nate became similar.

The nature of Drew's shift rotation now had him in contact with Nate far less frequently. Drew focused on his continued work on behaviour programs with residents on the open unit and consulting in team meetings. He went about his work as he always had, although he found himself feeling more and more apprehensive before his C Unit shift run. Nate was no longer the young man he knew and had interacted with; no longer the young man whose days he could make a little brighter. Drew still continued to gently approach Nate and make himself available. In response, Nate was either quiet or told Drew to fuck off. His ability to string those two words together had not diminished, and, perhaps because of the simplicity and clout of the phrase, it now represented the bulk of his verbal communication.

One evening, Nate sat facing the TV. Because it was quite late, the TV's sound was off, and many of his unit mates were into their quiet time or already asleep. Drew had a few moments to sit quietly in a chair at an angle to Nate. Joe, an older, completely hairless resident whose bed was located to Nate's immediate left, rose from his bed and began walking in bobbing circles around it. He patted the objects within the circumference of his reach with a trembling, Parkinsonian touch, and sometimes grunted. He eventually stopped and stood rigidly in a strange posture, elbows raised, forearms falling at 90 degrees. The sight of the scrawny man with his saggy, translucent skin floating in and around his hospital-issue underwear while standing in this odd position and staring vacantly would have been fully disturbing to those who weren't used to it. The staff and residents of C Unit were used to it – except for Nate.

Nate turned in the man's direction. "Head head I kick you in the head," he breathed quickly. "Head head I kick you in the head. I kick you in the head and now you're dead."

Drew saw no immediate potential for harm, but was inwardly alarmed by Nate's words in their content, rhyme, and rate. He was also alarmed by Nate's intense focus on the pale man.

"Head head I kick you in the head. I kick you in the head and now you're dead," breathed Nate again, the words grinding out through his clenched jaw.

Drew rose calmly and walked behind and around Nate over to Joe, softly encouraging Joe to lie down.

"Don't touch," said Nate, clearly and loudly. "Danger. I fix danger."

Joe settled into bed while Drew glanced slightly upward to his right to see that the team at the nursing station was well attentive to the situation. They were standing and awaiting any signal to intervene. He didn't call them off, but was also hoping he wouldn't have to call them out to the floor. He sat on the edge of the sofa between Nate and Joe's bunk and said, "That's Joe. He won't hurt you. He can't."

Nate was vibrating but still clinging to control. "Jack Jack his name is Jack." He snapped his head back and forced out a calming breath.

"Keep breathing, that's good," said Drew. "Cards or TV?" He reached behind him and pulled the deck of cards off the table to show Nate, in case Nate hadn't caught his words.

Nate's awareness reached the cards, but suddenly he appeared exhausted. "Or maybe bed?" asked Drew, hoping to plant the suggestion. Nate rose and walked away from Drew toward his bed. Another worker had appeared on the floor and stood with an easy posture by Nate's bunk as Nate retired, still breathing heavily.

Drew and Sam, the other worker, were greeted with visible curiosity when they reached the nursing station. "What was that?" asked Marty, the male nurse on duty that night.

"Who is Jack?" asked Drew.

No one on shift knew. While the scenario was somewhat unusual, no one on shift saw any cause for concern.

Drew charted his notes quickly at the end of his shift, and was happy that he was done his run on C Unit for a couple of weeks. However, he was never entirely free from it during his next run on the open unit. There was an increase in codes called on C Unit for a period. Drew couldn't help but believe that these were on account of a greatly agitated Nate.

Occasional flurries had been seen, often in mid-afternoon, floating on gentle winds and disappearing into the dark, not-yet-frozen river. Drew and his girlfriend were looking forward to a late fall trip to Ontario to visit her family. They were staying in the family "cottage," which was a massive log home in a ski community with a separate guest wing. They couldn't wait. While not having talked about it out loud, they also knew they would have to wait out the first few days of the family's anticipation of an engagement announcement, which wasn't coming. It was a subject that had become virtually absent in the couple's exchanges over the course of the fall. They were now oblivious to it, until faced with family. The ghost of their undefined future would haunt them for a few days, then fade into the wallpaper of routine.

Upon their return from vacation, Drew began a run of C Unit shifts. On his first night back, Drew helped tidy the common area, made his voice and smile a part of the residents' evening, and guided the able to the shower and back. He read a few pages of a John le Carré novel aloud to Barton. This was part of their routine when Drew was working. Barton, who was generally non-verbal, smiled and mouthed the words along with Drew. Drew then sat at the opposite end of the couch from Nate.

Nate was more heavily sedated than usual, having swung at a staff member early that morning. There was talk at a recent case conference of a transfer to IPI. Safety had become a consistent and pressing issue. On account of reduced exercise and increased medication, Nate had gained well over 50 pounds. His lethargy had not increased; instead, he had acquired more weight to throw behind his tackles and punches.

"Cards?" asked Drew, rotating the deck back and forth. Nate reached forward. As he was about to take the deck from Drew, Nate's gaze fixated somewhere behind Drew's head. His eyes went dark and his breathing became more rapid.

"You're dead dead I kicked you in the head," said Nate in a low voice. Confusion began to spread over his bloated features.

This didn't happen while I was gone? thought Drew, who couldn't recall reading anything relevant in Nate's chart at the start of the shift. The two remained facing each other on the couch. "That's Joe," Drew said evenly. "He is getting ready for bed. Joe can't hurt you."

"Jack head kicked in, I kicked it in, I kicked it in the river, I KICKED IT IN THE RIVER."

Nate stood and forgot about the couch directly behind him. He went to back away and fell over diagonally and awkwardly into a chair. This startled him. By the time he straightened himself, two other staff were down on the floor, making sure Joe was gone from Nate's sightline. Staring straight ahead, Nate began to make a strange, frightened noise, something between a closed-mouth scream and a howl. He leaned slowly forward, pouring himself off the chair and into a ball on the floor. Drew spoke with presence while keeping a safe distance. "We're here with you, Nate, we're here with you. It's safe here. We're here with you."

Drew repeated the words; he made and also repeated brief suggestions. Nate's level of agitation was rising even though he remained on the floor. Bonnie, who was the designated supervisor for the shift, came down from the station. She leaned her head toward the locked doors, indicating that Nate's and the others' needs were probably best served on this particular evening by a stay in one-to-one care. She retrieved the meds bag and followed the two other workers as they carefully raised Nate from the floor and guided him off of C unit. Nate was neither compliant nor resistant, but continued to howl through his locked jaw as he was led out.

Upon Bonnie's return to the unit, she and Drew went around with calming words and return to routine for any of the residents who showed any degree of residual agitation. Finally, they went back to the station.

"Who is Jack?" asked Drew, shaking his head.

Bonnie began to fill in the paperwork for the transfer. She paged the float team to bring in someone to attend to Nate.

"You ignoring me, old lady?" Drew asked, playfully.

"How about you pretend like you're the old lady and do some work?" quipped Bonnie with a light smile, not looking up from her paperwork.

"Who's Jack?" Drew asked again. "No one seems to know or care. But I don't think this is a mix-up in Nate's head."

She gave no response.

"Seriously," said Drew.

Bonnie realized he wasn't going to let it go. She put down her pen, took off her reading glasses, and wheeled her chair around to face Drew. Her features were unreadable. "Jack was his uncle."

In his mind, Drew flew through Nate's background information, which he had read two years previously when Nate was first admitted. "Pt was sexually abused and beaten repeatedly by father and uncle. This was disclosed after pt was put into foster care at age 14. Pt's father had abandoned pt and pt's brother, age 11. The brothers had been living alone in the family home for a month. Child Protection Services discovered pt and brother in a state of malnutrition, dehydration, and other neglect only after they had missed two weeks of school. Uncle was reported missing and was never found."

Drew began to shake his head and took a deep breath. He put his lips together and chewed on their insides. Gruesome, sad images took hold of his mind, and he shook his head more fervently. "He killed his uncle."

"Listen," said Bonnie. "That is not a known fact."

"It could be pretty easily figured out."

"You are creating a hypothesis."

"Bonnie, this would have been before the head trauma was extensive. He is spontaneously saying that he killed someone and disposed of a body – at age fourteen. Fourteen! He may have been a seriously dangerous person before –"

Bonnie moved in closer. "Drew. This is the deal. We work with facts. We work with what we have. We have a seriously brain injured, mentally ill young man who is in secure care, and inching his way toward a very early but very slow death."

"But who else wound up in a river? Who else got their head kicked in? Did some of the women he beat the shit out of wind up dead before they could get away from him? Everyone in this building has probably been in some degree of danger the whole time, more than we knew, a LOT more than we knew!" Drew put his head in his hands. He was having a hard time keeping it together. "Does Dr. Grigor know? Dr. Hoffman? Jolene?" He raised his head. "Did you?"

Bonnie saw Marty and Sam come through the doors on their way back from the one-to-one unit, chatting and laughing about something. She turned back to the phone, paged the float team again, then stood to address Drew. "You go straight to the staff lounge now. Do not pass go, do not collect two hundred dollars, do not speak to anyone. I will be there shortly."

Still beside himself, Drew shot off the chair past Bonnie. He nodded, tight-lipped, to Marty and Sam as they crossed paths in the doorway.

Fuck. Fuck, fuck, fuck, fuck, fuck, he said to himself as he stomped through the darkened corridors. The energy-efficient sensor lights came on one at a time ahead of him and then shut off behind him. His mind was spinning. The ghosts, the ghosts, he thought. Maybe nothing was as it seemed within what he had always felt to be the secure walls of the hospital, every aspect of which was designed for safety – or so he had thought. How many other people in here had done horrible, unaccounted-for things? How do you deal with these people, this kind of situation, this horribly misleading information? What hasn't happened to me? Drew stopped in his tracks in the hallway, feeling overwhelmed with nausea. In absence of motion, the lights all around him shut off. The darkness startled him back to into walking forward, jogging forward, then all but running to the staff room, where he opened a window for the full two inches it would open and stuck his face as far as he could into the cold air.

It seemed a long time before the door opened and Bonnie entered. She stood close to the door, giving him space. "So?" she asked.

He pulled his head in. "I don't know what to do," he said. Another wave of nausea hit and he put his face back to the window.

"Nothing is different," said Bonnie.

"What the hell?" yelled Drew, reeling to face her. "Everything is different!"

"To you, right now, probably."

"What is wrong with YOU?"

"Nothing," she said. "I am doing my job. I work with the patients I have. I work with the facts I have." She paused. "What would it change, Drew?"

He shook his head. "You knew."

Bonnie's words became directive. "I am also sending you home. You are white as a sheet and irrational, and clearly not well enough either physically or emotionally to continue working this evening." She approached the coat rack and patted Drew's jacket. "I don't have to accompany you, or have you accompanied." She paused. "Do I?"

Drew grabbed his jacket and marched past her. He didn't recall the drive home. Two hours later, his girlfriend returned from a movie and drinks night with her friends. She turned on the living room light and was startled to find Drew sitting in the dark, facing the balcony doors, which were wide open. "What is going on?" she asked slowly.

He couldn't bring himself to speak immediately. She came in and sat in the chair beside the couch. "What is it?" she asked.

A full minute passed. "I need to talk to you about something," he said.

She swallowed, then took a deep breath. "OK."

"I need to talk to you about a hypothetical ethical work situation."

She had to contain the laughter that wished to escape her on account of relief, and on account of her pending response. "You realize that I'm a criminal defence lawyer, right?"

"Exactly," he replied.

Drew excused himself from work for two weeks for medical reasons. He engaged the services of a highly experienced mentor and supervisor. Prior to returning to work, he met with Human Resources and asked to be removed from C Unit for an undetermined period of time, citing a personal conflict. No questions were asked. His C Unit hours were reallocated to working with management on policy development and the ongoing resident quality of care program. He thrived in the new role. He was now clean shaven and wore his hair slightly longer.

Bonnie retired at the end of the summer. The party was warm, slightly sad, and full of laughs. The relationship between Bonnie and Drew never quite recovered. Drew hugged her warmly on their way out from the gathering. In that moment, she spoke quickly of her faith in him, and wished him all the best. He wanted to thank her, but he couldn't.

It wasn't long before Nate was moved to IPI. Drew did not request a return to C Unit, and it was never offered.

The leaves displayed glorious fall colours, then floated to the ground, giving way to the grey of autumn. Afternoon flurries floated across streets and dissolved into the river.

Drew picked up his girlfriend from work a bit early, citing a work-related dinner function. As she climbed into the car, she saw his attire and asked, "Are you wearing a suit? What restaurant do we have around here where you seriously need to be wearing a suit?"

He shrugged. "It's a more dress-up type occasion."

"Nice of you to tell me."

"You always dress nice."

They drove to the old bridge down by the river. Since the new bridge had been built, this one was much quieter in terms of foot and vehicle traffic. "Where is this restaurant?" she asked. "I'm kind of excited. Is it new?"

He stopped the car. "Come on. I want to show you something."

He took her hand and they walked to the highest point of the bridge's arch. It was overcast. Flurries danced around them as the sky darkened with day's end. The sound of the river against the struts of the bridge drowned out any distant sounds of traffic. It felt as though they were in another place altogether. He stopped and turned to face her, taking both of her hands in his. She could feel the velvet texture of a small box between her right hand and his left.

"Marry me," he said, smiling like she had never seen him smile.

Islands

Diesel fumes, constant rocking, and the scent of not-quite-successful deck cleaning had Jane Horowitz tightening her throat, swallowing a lot, and staring straight ahead at the approaching island. Can you not get bigger, faster, she thought. Bigger meant the ferry ride would be almost over.

Go to the island, they said. It will do you good, they said.

With Jane freshly discarded from a two-year relationship, her friends begged her to keep her holiday time. Book something else, for God's sake, Jane, but go. She was on the fence about it. If it hadn't been for Ben's obsession with what seemed to be his one and only bucket list item, a week in Las Vegas, she never would have booked any time off at all. Jane only ever booked holidays as adjuncts to business trips in order to save money. She had never chosen a destination. Her vacations were never self-sufficient ideas.

Bearpaw Island was not entirely Jane's self-sufficient idea, either. She had been at a total loss for a place to spend her time during the defunct Vegas week, although she knew her friends were right and she should get away for a bit. At least Bearpaw sort of felt like her own idea, since she had actually thought of it herself once, albeit as a child. Studying the province's geography in fifth grade, her eyes kept moving to the left bottom corner of the map and a little island named for its shape. It was known for its world-renowned contemporary painting community, contrasted with an equally well-known and impeccably preserved display of First Nations artefacts and early clothing. That would be a neat place, she had thought. In adulthood, Jane learned of the island's excellent microbrewing company and a legendary hole-in-the-wall pub. A Michelin-starred chef had retired to work there. A trip to Bearpaw would not remotely resemble her middle-class, middle-of-the-road, more-or-less comfortable upbringing and subsequently similar adult life. It was as win-win as a reluctant vacation was going to get.

Two years' worth of a relationship with Ben had been enough to cause awkwardness, distress, loss of routine, and broken connections with new friends and family. It was not long enough to cause the level of horror and heartache that she had known on a previous occasion because of a breakup. She was fine, and knew she was going to be. She was thirty-eight years old; Ben was not her first rodeo. Meanwhile, it was all the "whys" and "what ifs" and "who was this person all along, really" that she was stuck with. Cognitive problems. Cognitive problems that ate too much of her time and frequently left her eating too much ice cream before bed.

She admittedly had a lot of cognitive problems. But she had promised herself, while on this trip, to either face them full on or leave them stuffed in her suitcase while she put in an afternoon on a steep hiking trail. Both tactics were in sharp contrast to the in-between that had defined, or rather failed to define, most of her days.

'Forget Beh-eh-ehn,' she sang to herself in her head. She blinked and noted the land mass to be much larger now. Cliffs and inlets were defined. There were banks of shadow and sunlight, and she felt that she might actually someday warm up. She had chosen three hours out on the main deck over three hours of indoor nausea exacerbated by the smell of fried food.

Lots of metallic and industrial sounds, along with shouting and pointing from a few sunburnt men in loud safety vests, signalled the start of the disembarkation process. Jane barely remembered climbing aboard the boat to begin with, and had observed little of the companion vehicles around her. As they moved off and along, she saw a fairly balanced mix of vacationers, delivery and service vehicles, residents returning home, and retired seniors. Jane had been any and all of these people, at one time or another, except the seniors. Jesus, she thought to herself. That's next. She began to imagine all the impediments seniors would have while travelling. Frequent bathroom stops. Forgetfulness of directions. Leaving things behind in motels. Leaving –

Stuff it, she thought. Cognitive problem. Stuff it.

It was a 45-minute drive from the terminal to her cabin reservation in Brigg's Cove. The cabin had been a significant splurge. Each unit was uniquely built into the cliff structure. In deliberate contrast to the Dwell Magazine-like architecture, the décor was complete and utter kitsch. It had looked spectacular in the online photos. On top of the lodging itself, hiking trails that ran from one end of the island to the other cut through the upper end of the property. It was the antithesis of every chain hotel she had ever stayed at, of which there had been a solid number. The drive to the cove was pretty, and she noted the location of a small grocery store and pharmacy along the way, as well as a few boutiques where she might stop sometime during the week.

Jane parked at the building that had OFFICE spelled across the top of the door in an unlit neon sign circa 1960. There was a note taped to the inside of the window on the door, informing her that the owners were out, and the key was in her cabin. And to have a Great Brigg Experience! Ohhh my God, she whispered under her breath.

She got back in her car and slowly climbed the narrow, winding gravel road to #6.

The cabin did not disappoint. A good half of it lay nestled into the cliffside; the primary building material emerging from the rock was glass. Vertical beams of rough wood held the tall, crystal-clear walls together. The cabin was situated 40 feet from a sheer drop. Jane was floored by a view of rolling fog, choppy waves, and seals.

The interior kitsch factor made the website photos look stale and boring. Giant hooked rugs depicted scenes such as self-satisfied pink poodles playing polo on horseback, and stick figure families enjoying a 1950s-style picnic while oblivious to the giant bear who lurked behind a tree with an evil, drooling grin. The closet held a staged collection of the worst handbags she had ever seen. There were three epically strange clocks in each room, always one with too many moving parts. That bit exceeded her threshold for kitsch, crossing well over into the realm of creepy. She felt she might have to rearrange the clock situation for the week. The lamps were from the 1950s, and gaudy. None of the dishes or cutlery matched. Ostentatious yet clean throws of white sheepskin and neon zebra patterns lay draped over the furniture. Over the mantle of the fireplace hung a magnificent, giant velvet painting of a cougar draped over a grand piano while holding a martini. The bed linens were impeccable. Jane was pleased at the deliberate mess.

She itched to get at a trail. However, there was no question of getting groceries and amenities prior to possibly enjoying anything further.

She returned to her car and doubled back the short distance to the little town and parked at the grocery store. The absence of other cars in the parking lot was shortly explained by a note taped to the door: BACK LATER

Jane frowned and walked across the way to the cute A-frame cabin which was the pharmacy. She was consumed by the premonition that she was about to read a similar sign; except this time, there was no sign at all. The lights were on inside, but the door was locked.

She drove a half-mile further back toward the pier and was rewarded with a closed hardware store. Its absentee signage consisted of a "Back In ..." faded blue plastic clock whose light red hands had been moved to a time that made no sense at all, given the current hour. Jane's brow furrowed. She sighed and got back into her car, wondering if she had hit the Canadian equivalent of siesta time in Spain, and tried to decide what her next move would be. This was her vacation. Hers. In a place that was the Anti-Vegas, and becoming moreso by the minute. She tried not to be annoyed, and felt herself failing miserably. She was losing out on precious –

I'll take a drive, she thought. Then: Why don't you just go hiking? Because if I go hiking, then everything will be closed by the time I get back, and I'll be hungry and won't have anything to start tomorrow off, either, and it will all be wasted time like even more than right now –

"Cognitive problems," she warned herself out loud. A drive it is.

Jane continued out past Brigg's on a winding coastal road, which dipped to sea level and remained there, following the shoreline. It was flat compared to the drive inland from the ferry. She found herself zoning out until she saw a striking sign, beautifully hand-carved in wood, that read BEARPAW PUB & BREWERY. It woke her from her grey funk of dismay and she swung the car at the last minute to make the turn.

The layout of the business's location was amazingly artful. The buildings had been smartly situated and spaced within the clearing. The walkways through the industrial silos and storage units past the brewery buildings were wonderfully thought-out, gently guiding the visitor to a narrow path through the woods leading out to the pub. Although it was not currently illuminated, Jane could see how lighting had been set up to make the walk into an experience unto itself at night. She felt hopeful as she walked down the path. A few empty cars sat in the parking area. She had an almost primal need to feel as though she had accomplished something today. And what was more Canadian of an accomplishment than picking up beer on a Sunday? She found herself smiling slightly. She never would have considered this an accomplishment back home.

A person! thought Jane, watching a kitchen employee with a huge mess of hair and beard wheeling a cart of vegetables and disappearing around the back of the pub. It was the first human she had laid eyes on since her fellow ferry passengers had branched off onto various side roads. She walked up the stairs onto the wrap around deck of the pub and found herself looking at a view of the water that was entirely different, yet just as spectacular, as the view from her cabin. There was no note or faded plastic clock on the door, which was open. What sort of pub would be closed in the middle of the afternoon at the start of tourist season, anyway?

Yet, the incredible pub, with its nooks and crannies for days and old church benches and memorabilia and tokens left behind by tourists from around the globe and its canoe paddles turned into light fixtures and its giant wall of high end spirits and its seemingly endless lineup of taps was, like everything else on the island so far in Jane's day, closed. No music. No active electricity. Not operational. She stood incredulously for a moment, feeling both privileged to have arrived at the legendary pub and discouraged by her continued lack of advancement. Why was this bothering her so much? She had chosen to vacation at a remote location. Alone. It was, however, becoming painfully true that neither of these had ever really been her intention for the trip. She exhaled slowly with the realization, and turned to leave.

"Hello?" said a voice behind her, accompanied by the sound of swinging saloon doors.

Jane turned to face the mess of a man she had seen pushing the cart of vegetables earlier. She was slightly taken aback by his handsomeness, albeit in a whitely hirsute, 60-year-old package. "Sorry we're not open yet," he said.

"Par for the course," said Jane.

The man laughed. "Your first time on the island. Not too much happens between noon and three."

"What do people do?" Jane asked, unable to mask the incredulousness and mild annoyance that she still felt.

He shrugged. "Whatever they want."

She shook her head. "I could never get away with that," she said.

"Why not?"

"Why not?" she replied. "Most of the world couldn't."

"This isn't most of the world."

"Sure isn't." Jane shook her head, wondering why she was being so brutal. She prepared to apologize and leave.

The man took a good look at her and made an appraisal. Then he reached under the bar for two glasses, and behind the bar for a bottle of scotch. The label was unfamiliar to Jane. He poured generously and set one glass closer to her on the bar. "Your name?" he asked.

"Jane."

"Last name?"

"Horowitz."

"Jewish?"

"No. My father was a disinterested Jew. My mother was a tradition-clinging but non-practicing Catholic. Anyway. And you? Your name is …"

"Ben."

She closed her eyes. "No."

Ben laughed out loud again. It was a rapid, fun sound. "No? I would beg to differ."

Jane reeled herself in. She approached the bar and took the glass. "Thanks," she said to the man, and sipped gently. The richness and dimension of the scotch struck her immediately. A beautiful blend of smoke and spice lingered. "Oh wow," she said, grounded by the luxurious expanse of the drink. She began to breathe. "Campbeltown? Islay?" she asked, more to herself than to her new acquaintance as she attempted to divine the drink's origin. She liberally took a large mouthful before starting anew with the kind stranger. "Ben is the name of my ex," she explained more gently, "with whom I am supposed to be on vacation in Vegas right now, except for the little impediment of our sudden breakup."

"I'm sorry to hear that," he said, with decent sincerity. He pulled a stool from a corner, sat down, and made a subtle gesture for her to do the same on the other side of the bar. She did so. "You do realize that you're not in Vegas," he said, his smile charming and coy.

She nodded slowly. "Well aware," she said.

"So what made you choose this end of the spectrum for your time?" he asked.

"Well … all the things you're faced with when you get dumped for a younger model, really. What am I doing. What am I doing wrong. Etc., etc. And – " It can't be the drink already, she thought, hearing her continued honesty spoken aloud before she could stop herself. " – I was captivated by this place when I was little." Oh my God, stop talking, she thought.

"Hmmm," he said.

Jane shook her head. "I'm sorry. You work here. I am interrupting you. What do you do?"

The man had chosen to be entertained by Jane's floundering instead of defaulting to offendedness. He smiled again and slowly looked up, a gesture to the space above the wall of spirits behind him. Jane followed his eyes to a mounted series of photos of Benjamin Nordstrom, albeit with far better grooming. There he was in full chef's regalia and a leading man's smile, shaking hands with the likes of Gordon Ramsay, Justin Trudeau, Angelina Jolie, Jodie Foster, David Schwimmer, Michael Phelps, Anthony Bourdain, Eugenie Bouchard, Michael Imperioli, Ryan Gosling, Sarah MacLachlan – and those were only the ones she recognized immediately.

"Oh my God," she said. "Ohhhhhh my God." Jane put her entire head in her hands. "You're the other reason I chose to come here ... other than my Grade Five obsession with First Nations things." Jane was fully back to earth and entirely mortified. She lifted her hands and set them back on the bar. She sank the rest of her scotch and slowly began to rise. "I am so sorry. I'm a total idiot. I'll ... let you get back to work."

"You think I'm offended?" he asked.

"I would be, if this was reversed," she said. "I'm so sorry. So. Yeah. I'm gonna head out now."

"I would actually be offended if you left." He opened the bottle and refilled her glass. "Have one more drink with me. Please. I'm not asking out of politeness."

This intrigued her somewhat and helped her get past herself a little, which was a welcomed feeling, as getting past herself was proving to be a pervasive problem.

"You would be surprised at how much that happens to me now," he said. "It was actually one of the reasons I came here. This isn't a place you get to by chance. Although a lot of wonderful chance happens here." He paused. "Perhaps that's part of what you're looking for?"

"I didn't realize I was looking for anything," she said, "aside from keeping my mind off of where I was supposed to be. And wanting some world-class beer and food."

"And how's all that going for you?" He smiled and swirled the lovely liquid around in his glass. He watched it cling to the sides of the glass and fall slowly to the bottom. "Jane Horowitz, my new friend, people come to Bearpaw for one of two reasons: to relax and get away from it all, and read a lot of books; or to throw themselves to chance, and start off in whatever new direction they happen to land. There isn't much in-between. The artist community here may be multigenerational now, but they are all still living for chance. They live for the random and intuitive happenings around them, and for the random and intuitive happenings within them. Even the senior set that comes here – I guess I am one of them, now – they too are giving themselves over to chance."

The drink had helped her get her land legs back. She hadn't realized that they were still missing from the ferry ride. "That was among your reasons?" she asked.

"Absolutely. Because when you lose sight of chance, you stop creating for creation's sake, and you start dying as an artist. And as a person." He held her eyes while she looked back at his, under the incredible lineup of photos above him. "I had come full circle. I was dying." He finished his own drink, and rose from the stool. "Which reminds me. As you observed earlier, I do still have a job." Jane rose from her seat as well. "Can I be honest with you, Jane Horowitz? I don't know what it is, but I feel I can be honest with you."

Chance was all she felt she had going for her at this point. "Sure," she said, almost as a question.

"You waited until you got dumped just shy of turning forty to indulge the dream of a little girl. Somehow along the way, you slipped into keeping things predictable and reigned-in all the time. You probably never get speeding tickets because you're never late for anything. You've made an incredibly safe and boring island of yourself. No one is visiting, or is even really able to visit. You turned your back on chance a long time ago. Stop walking in the middle of the road. The little passion you have admittedly allowed yourself for food and booze is allowing me to feel some hope for you."

Jane was trying not to fall over, or cry, or both.

He collected the glasses and set them down beneath the bar. "Directness comes with my territory," he said, the afterthought skirting apology. He then visibly switched gears. "We open at four each day."

It took her a moment to find her voice. "Thank you."

"Try to have fun," he said. And then he grinned the grin that she expected had charmed thousands of women, customers, celebrities, employers, employees, good friends, and complete strangers over the years. "That is, until you no longer have to try." He turned and headed out back beyond the saloon doors. She watched as the doors swung back and forth, until they didn't.

Of all the people, she thought to herself. Because she got dumped, because she had actually listened to her friends, because she had actually listened to herself. Because she read note after note stating that people were busy elsewhere today; because the plastic hands of a fake clock were set to a time far before or beyond the hour she essentially never lived in.

Jane walked back to her car. She felt more disoriented than she had in her entire life. I'm a mess, she thought. I'm actually a legit mess.

She headed back to the cabin and sat for some time, staring at the rug with the pink poodle polo match, the eyes of the poodles impossibly yet contentedly closed and their smug joy represented by thin black mouth lines, turned up just so slightly at the ends. She briefly wondered if she would be able to follow, to any degree, the barren directive that had been given to her. All she really knew was that she was staring at a bizarre hooked rug. And that, during the entire time she stared at it, she had no cognitive problems at all.

Transformers

"Where are we going, Daddy?"

"Same place we always go, only different."

With reassurance, Ren looked up into the rear view mirror and into his son's eyes, inverted. They were in was a new neighbourhood today. Bradley didn't recognize it. Neither did Ren, but it wasn't Bradley's job to work it out.

Bradley seemed neither content with nor distressed by the response. He continued to explore the scenery of the industrial park from the secure position of his booster seat.

A bus terminal, a textiles plant, a restaurant equipment store, a collision service, a wayward sausage cart on a corner. A commercial laundry facility, a bulk distributor of outdated office furnishings.

There it was: A-1 Paper Products. Second entrance, the text said. Around to the back, park 20 feet from the door no closer than the dent six feet up the sheet metal siding.

Ren put the car in park and waited as instructed between 10 and 15 minutes. Sometime between 10 and 15 minutes later, a man whose face was barely visible under the hood of his winter coat appeared behind the car and then alongside the driver's door. Ren brought the window down. "Things are good?" a voice asked from within the hood.

Ren nodded. He brought the window back up and opened the door slightly. Keeping his hands low, he gave something to the man and received something in return. Neither cameras nor Bradley could ever see what was exchanged. "Things are great," replied Ren. "Have a great Tuesday."

"You too."

The man retraced his steps and disappeared. Ren waited between 10 and 15 minutes. Then he reversed along the exact path by which he had entered. The drive resumed through similar but different structures along the long, wide road of the industrial park.

"Tuesday, Tuesday Tuesday Tuesday," Bradley sang in a made-up song to himself. "It's never Tuesday, never never never never –"

"Hungry?" asked Ren through the rear view mirror.

"Yeah!" yelled Bradley with a big smile, raising his arms awkwardly within the confines his puffy snowsuit and the gross motor skills of a child that was four-and-a-half years old.

It was their regular visit to McDonalds, albeit never the same McDonalds in a row. Ren extracted Bradley from the snowsuit and set him up with his Transformer in the booth nearest to the order counter.

"Where's my Happy Meal?" asked Bradley with all seriousness as Ren returned with a tray devoid of the magic box.

Ren shook his head with the same level of seriousness. "No Transformer toys. Only Mario toys."

Bradley nodded and reached for a french fry, which amounted to a handful of fries. "Good job, Daddy."

"Eat slow if you want some time in Playplace."

"Okay. I can do it."

Bradley trundled off to Playplace while Ren collected winter garments and garbage. He relocated to a bench just outside the glassed-in area where he could keep an eye on Bradley and check his phone. THURSDAY IN LOWELL read the only text.

A sinking feeling of fear and disappointment congealed along with the mound of partially digested fast food in Ren's stomach. Outwardly, he crossed his legs, leaned back casually, and slipped his phone back into his winter vest pocket. He waited between 10 and 15 minutes, and then tapped lightly on the glass of the play area. Then again on the glass. Then he began to move toward the Playplace door, which sent Bradley scrambling out from under a pile of multicoloured balls to meet his father.

"Don't we go home now?" asked Bradley as they took the exit onto the perimeter highway. The fan blasted semi-warm air onto the windshield. Ren shivered a bit and patted the passenger seat in search of his gloves.

"We do," he said, keeping his eyes on the highway. "We have to do one more favour first."

"Where?"

"Not far. You'll know the neighbourhood."

"What is it?"

"You tell me when you see it."

"Okay. I can do it."

"Good man. Tell me when you know."

Before long, they left the highway and entered a subdivision, which seemed neither poor nor affluent. It was a collection of small wartime houses had been renovated in attempts to resemble more upscale housing. They remained small, wartime houses with expensive windows and siding in trendy colours. Ren never liked this neighbourhood. It was a pile of pretend to him.

"Lowell!" yelled Bradley, waving his arms.

Ren smiled despite himself. "That's right! Good job."

They advanced down a side street where the same type of houses appeared, only this time they were run-down; free from the unsuccessful makeovers featured just around the corner. At the cul-de-sac, Ren turned the car around and parked in front of the second last house on the right. He took his phone out of his vest pocket, sent a quick text message, and looked sideways to the living room window with its curtains fully drawn. The curtains moved slightly.

The sound of a door slamming sent Ren into high alert. He saw nothing right away. Then a giant man with wild eyes came stomping as fast as a giant man can from around the back of the house and in the direction of the car. There was no 10 to 15 minute rule to be had in Lowell today. The man crunched across the dirty snow in his sock feet, carrying a sledgehammer. It looked like a regular hammer against the background of his massive torso.

Ren put the car in gear and sped off just as Bradley saw the man approaching and began to cry in fear. The boy howled and howled. Ren looked in the rear view mirror not at his son, but at the shoeless man in a white undershirt who spun toward the house and threw the sledgehammer overhand through the living room window, his mouth a gaping hole of inaudible rage.

The car rounded a corner. Ren found his voice and began to speak soothingly to his son, and somewhat to himself. "We're OK," he heard himself say, surprised by the calm of his tone. "I don't know who that man was, but he wasn't supposed to be there. He wasn't mad at us. We'll never see him again." He took an unusual route home, talking the whole time in the hopes that Bradley wouldn't notice.

Ren knew exactly who the man was. The man was Cletus Dockerty, and he was entirely supposed to be there. Over the past year, Ren had somehow managed to escape any and all calls to Dockerty's place. A Thursday call was never guaranteed to be a safe one. But a Thursday call to Dockerty's was known to end in complete oblivion, or injury, or both. The injury today was to little Bradley. Bradley was never to bear the brunt of Ren's work. Ever. Ren fought the twisting in his gut as he continued to talk to his son, who, exhausted, finally fell asleep close to their home.

As the garage door descended behind the car, Ren snapped out of parent mode and suddenly reached for his phone. He had been too wrapped up in Bradley to check his messages. The sole message read: ONE MORE = ORPHAN

He was shockingly unfazed by the threat on his life. He had been expecting such a message since the one other time he had missed a favour on account of concern for Bradley's safety. Then a feeling of dread began to rise. He pushed it down and lifted Bradley from the backseat, holding him tightly to his chest. Bradley continued to sleep, tears and snot now dried all over the front of his snowsuit. Father and son moved as one being around the front of the car. Ren disabled the alarm, and climbed the steps up to the door that opened into the kitchen.

The house was dark, quiet, calm. It was sparse but comfortable in its furnishings. A variety of toys lay in one corner of the living room; a workbench hosting a pile of small tools and a couple of dissembled computers stood in the other. The workbench represented neither a hobby nor a job. It was part of the set on which Ren played the role of Computer Guy, which was the job he spoke of when asked what his job was. He crossed the living room to the bedroom that he shared with Bradley. He cleaned up his son, put him in his favourite and warmest pyjamas, and tucked him snugly into bed. An emoji nightlight of a happy face with its eyes closed glowed from an outlet at the foot of the little bed. Bradley wiggled and stretched as his father kissed him goodnight.

"We home, Daddy?"

Ren nodded and rubbed Bradley's chest. "We sure are."

"Will tomorrow be like today? I didn't like today. Where are we going tomorrow?"

"Well, buddy ..." Ren paused to gather some confidence for his voice. "How do you feel about finding a new house?"

"I like when we find a new house," murmured Bradley. Sleep was on the verge of returning. Before he was gone again, he asked, "You said Mommy's not coming back, right? She won't have to try to find us?"

Ren swallowed hard. Mommy was absolutely not coming back. "No. You don't have to worry about that. It's just you and Daddy now, together, all the time."

Bradley was asleep before Ren finished his last sentence. Ren headed out into the living room, where he fished another phone out from within one of the skeletal computers. He set up a trailer rental under an assumed name. He went out to the garage, changed out the plates on the car, and replaced the insurance and registration cards. He went back into the house and took inventory of the closets. These contained boxes that were props on the set of his existence, filled with made-up memorabilia, fake family photos, and seldom used household items. The boxes were perpetually packed for the sole purpose of creating the illusion of a family's moving day.

Tomorrow was moving day now. For a moment, Ren felt completely disoriented, having no idea of what day of the week tomorrow actually was.

Campy Birthday

On Highway 112, a collector road that forged through alternating patches of dense woods and open farmland somewhere between Town X and Village Y, a small family farm was situated approximately 15 kilometres in. THE SAUERS, stated the sign, below which there was a second, much newer swinging wood-burned plank that read: B&B.

It was an unlikely spot for a B&B. But there it was, a quaint, slightly run-down 1800s-era farmhouse that offered some sort of authentic experience, should one wish to roll the dice on a getaway, or on a late night exhaustion-fuelled stop, or to simply roll the dice.

Laetitia Sauer closed the hall closet door on another day of vacuuming. On her way to the kitchen, she grabbed the vase that typically sat atop the reception counter in order to refill it with the flowers she had collected walking in the fields that day. Lupins. Daisies. Buttercups. Lilac. Some other things that she had no idea what they were, nor did it matter. She refreshed the vase with wildflowers and water, and walked it back to its station on the counter. She verified that the rest of the counter was in order, and did the same for the contents of the entryway. This included the "guest" book, with its most recent signatures. These were, in fact, mostly from her own hand.

She found herself wandering to one of the kitchen chairs. She sat, looking outside at the deepening twilight. She waited for her brothers and sisters to awaken.

Normally, they unfolded themselves from beneath the floorboards of the barn in the field one by one and eventually floated up to the farmhouse. On this particular evening, they all crashed in through the back door together. There would be guests tonight for the first time in weeks. Frequencies of excitement and hunger emanated from all four siblings.

The remaining children of German immigrants Dobret and Hilda Sauer were twins Tracy and Tammy, and their respectively older and oldest brothers, Todd and Tank (whose real name was Terrence). In the awkward stage of early awakening, combined with significant agitation from days of hunger, the four vibrated with a slight degree of disorientation just inside of the kitchen door. The door, which did not operate on a spring, closed itself behind them.

"What time do they check in?" asked Todd. He was gently bouncing and swaying from side to side. His arms were folded across his now perpetually scrawny body, and he scratched at the skin of his opposite elbows.

"They said nine. They might be later," replied Laetitia, rolling the stem of a spare daisy between her fingers and thumb.

Laetitia was the youngest sibling by seven years. She was technically 24, but was 17 when she was transformed from human to inhuman. Laetitia possessed the phenomenally rare trait of being able to live by day as well as by night. She was one in a billion, a passing visitor had told the siblings once. The visitor had looked at Laetitia with longing and unmistakable hatred. He told the family to protect their priceless asset, just before flying out the open kitchen window in the form of an elongated fingerprint.

The siblings thought this was quite the joke. They had been plotting for some time to remove Laetitia permanently from their lives, simply out of what seemed to be irreconcilable differences stemming from the power imbalance. In the coming days, they were inundated with flock after flock of undead itinerants who had clearly heard of the "asset", and subsequently came in the night to try to steal it. The sibling DNA in the Sauers got fired up instinctually, and many a stake went through many an unbeating heart for a solid year before word finally got around that the Sauer crew was not to be fucked with. Finally, the sulci and gyri of the siblings' strange brains began to wrap themselves around the concept of their little sister's extraordinary value. Social camouflage. Food made available night AND day. The best of both worlds provided within the confined shadows of their own. They snapped out of it then. And they transformed the interrupted family farm into two new enterprises altogether: a canned corn packaging facility, as this could operate easily both day and night; and a bed and breakfast for the largely unfortunate.

Largely unfortunate? Indeed. Only two types of guests frequented such a removed B&B. The first type consisted of thirty-somethings en route to somewhere else, who remained connected to everyone and everything via social media. The second consisted of people who were totally screwed and running from something, and therefore seeking the opposite of connectivity. The former, unless they appeared perfectly unplugged, left the premises in the morning as Laetitia waved goodbye from the selfie-esque front deck. The latter did not get to see Laetitia waving from the front deck. And, sometimes, when the Sauers got lucky, some sick and vengeful schmuck came the way of Highway 112, on the collector road somewhere between Town X and Village Y, looking for the screwed and the running. Generally, this represented a very good day for the Sauers.

Laetitia looked up from the daisy between her fingers to the portrait of her parents on their wedding day in 1965. It was a large, faded colour artifact in an oversized, oval-shaped frame, and was more reminiscent of a funeral portrait than of a wedding one. It hung too high above an armoire that contained two things: ancient European silverware that was of no interest to the children, but probably worth a fair amount of money; and industrial cleaning supplies.

"You guys are too hungry," she said to her siblings. "You're being creepy. You might want to let me sort this one out."

"How the hell are you not a total mess right now?" asked Tammy, with an impulsivity that was not atypical for her. "You haven't eaten since we last did."

"You guys won't do the frozen smoothies," said Laetitia. "You're too good for that, apparently. Meanwhile, I get to go to town all the time and buy groceries I can never eat." She paused for a second. "The smoothies aren't all that bad, you guys."

All four siblings resumed agitation, and stomped around the kitchen.

"Well." Laetitia rose. "I'd best go put my contacts in."

Tank laughed out loud. His square-shaped self looked squarely at his favourite and youngest sister. "I hadn't even noticed 'til now. Yeah, please. Go do that."

Laetitia smiled and headed to the back quarters of the house where she slept. She had long managed the art of putting in contact lenses without a mirror. Her vision was 20/20, and would remain so in perpetuity. But her irises were white. This was another feature of her uniqueness. However, this feature wouldn't do on the face of a commercial-corn-production-slash-quaint-country-accommodations enterprise. Unable to look in a mirror since the tender age of 17, she had no idea what sort of oddity she might really look like with her white eyes. Tank had taken a picture once, to give her an idea. She hated everything she saw in the picture on a cellular level. She would rather have experienced the burn of the mirror. Enter the internet, and an online prescription for coloured contact lenses. Tank had taken a second picture. She thought she looked much better, but couldn't reconcile the image of these falsely coloured eyes as her own any more than she could reconcile that of the grotesque white ones. However, at this particular moment, she didn't give a thought to anything except the procedure of placing the contacts. She re-emerged just as the sound of tires meeting gravel came closer to the house. Of course, they had all first heard this when the car was still a full kilometre away.

"Get out of here!" she hissed at her siblings. Reluctantly, they filed out the back door and snapped into the shape of bats against the backdrop of mid-summer dusk. This better enabled them to watch the activity through the windows.

Laetitia looked up again briefly at the portrait of her parents. A pang of guilt and sadness always passed through her just before she greeted "guests" at the family home. This wasn't what was supposed to be, or who she was supposed to be.

Her parents were not invited to preternatural life by those who had re-invented the rest of the family. Those creatures been invited to the Sauer family home by an unknowing Todd late one night following a party, during what was to be his final drug binge. Todd had made years of errors in personal and social judgement leading up to this most terrible one. Todd's newest (and last) "friends" were the children of locals who had hated the Sauer children simply for being cared for. For being set for life with a family business. For being mostly good at sports, academically successful, known in the village as super nice people; all the things the visitors' parents had failed to provide for them on account of sketchy and poorly managed drug enterprises. Their own shitty, earthly lives were stolen by a group of unknown partiers. And now, having less than nothing to lose, Todd's entourage for the night wanted nothing more than for the seemingly perfect Sauer children to feel as isolated as they had, and forever. And so, Dobret and Hilda Sauer were tied to the chairs of the dining room table and made to watch their children die and live, one by one. The father's life was then ended, the mother's immediately following. For some reason, perhaps to remove any chance of closure from the younger Sauers, the creatures left with the bodies of the parents. This had always disturbed the siblings. They never spoke of it collectively. They all thought of it frequently.

Laetitia, now left alone, took a deep breath and practiced her smile, sans mirroir. She imagined how her permanently long, wavy blond hair might look, pulled back as it always was into a loose ponytail. The quintessential farm girl. She did not feel fully pleased with her smile, so she made some adjustments, and headed toward the door.

"Hello there!" she said to the barely 20-something couple, who was clearly from a bigger city and wanting to try something novel. They pulled their little carry-on airline luggage behind them as they stepped onto the porch and marvelled among themselves about how cool this place was in real life. They barely acknowledged Laetitia as they took selfies, separately and together, and paused while attempting to post things.

"Hey!" they said together, in greeting. The male followed up with: "Your wifi isn't working and we have no signal."

Laetitia had never quite seen this particular couple at the homestead. They were much younger than usual. If they were trying their best to appear as though they had no money, they had failed spectacularly. Their haircuts, his barber-trimmed facial hair, and their expensive scents gave them away. That, and the brazenly ignorant attitude that oozed from them.

"Oh no," said Laetitia laboriously, with her best effort at empathy. "The router shorted out and we're waiting on a new one."

A common story. "Plus, we're pretty far in the woods out here. We have signal at summer solstice." She laughed, finding herself funny. Hearing the words out loud, she realized they weren't at all funny. Comedy had never been her strong suit.

"Shit," wondered the male to the female, visibly put off by and somewhat fearful of the lack of connectivity, particularly the free kind. "Do you think we can stay? Can we do it?"

The female shrugged and then looked cunningly toward the male. "It'll be the best! We'll have so much to post later!" she almost screamed, with a giant smile. "Best night ever! Already!"

"Sure! Great!" He laughed with relief and grabbed both of the female's hands. He almost addressed Laetitia directly. "Which room are we in? Do you want payment now or in the morning?"

Laetitia's mouth found her practiced smile. "Morning is fine," she said. She asked them what they might like for breakfast. This all felt hollow. She had a strong feeling that she had wasted money on groceries. And that she would pull money from one of their carry-ons the next day rather than politely taking it from their warm hands as she said goodbye. She didn't have the reason yet. She would wait. She waited so much better than her siblings. This, aside from their blatant hunger, was the other reason she had sent them packing earlier. "Let me show you to your room."

"Look at this! Wait, THIS! Oh-em-gee LOOK over here!" The couple had returned exclusively to their own company and were lapping up the décor of the house, which had not changed since the family's transformation. "There's stuff in German!" almost shouted the female. Her voice was always on the brink of shouting.

Jesus Christ, thought Laetitia. It was the first time she had sworn to herself in years. She had begun to feel what she faintly recalled as irritation.

The young woman had moved on to the portrait of Dobret and Hilda Sauer on their wedding day, in which the newlyweds had permitted themselves a set of pleased but toothless smiles. "Check THIS out!" she semi-howled, grabbing her boyfriend's shirt-sleeve and pointing upward. "Look how they're almost happy! How SEVENTIES is this picture?? I LOVE this!" She leapt into his arms.

He laughed and swung her around once, put her down, and then said, "Ha ha, right? Soooo campy."

Her face was aglow with excitement. "Campy Birthday to me!" she yelled. So this was the reason for the season. The couple laughed together and then turned to Laetitia, ready to meet their room.

Instead, they met their own death.

Over the last fifteen seconds, Laetitia's faint stirrings of irritation had fireballed into a horrific mix of grief and rage. With the comments about her parents, she no longer saw the two individuals standing in her family home as human beings. They were now sustenance, and a sick, illogical, unstoppable opportunity for an act of revenge. Nothing like this had happened to her since the siblings established the bed and breakfast. She didn't care. She registered the terror of the guests, and snapped to action during their split second of paralysis.

She kicked the female in the chest, sending her into the armoire and then to the ground. While the woman floundered, Laetitia whipped a chair away from the table and bound the man to it with the tablecloth. The dated yet impeccable place settings crashed to the floor around them. Before the female could fully catch her breath to get up, Laetitia grabbed another chair, picked the female up by the collar of her shirt, and smashed her body down into the chair. Laetitia breathed deeply. She was on the strangest trajectory she had known in years, and was entirely caught up in the rush that went with it. She fixed her eyes on the female guest, who had begun to cry.

"I can't feel my legs," she choked out between sobs and breaths. Her torso and arms were moving around as if entirely detached from her hips and everything below.

The male found his voice and began to yell. Laetitia swooped in and drained him instantly. He fell limp and lifeless into the table-cloth that surrounded him. The female found her voice and began to scream. Laetitia wheeled, and the gaze that lit upon the female silenced her instantly. Even so, her mouth remained open, her neck long, her vocal cords taught.

Calmed by the initial feed, Laetitia walked slowly toward the female, who continued to writhe from the working upper half of her body. She screamed in perfect silence, a warped baby bird. Laetitia popped out her contact lenses and smiled at the woman. The writhing became furious. Laetitia bared her teeth and dove for the woman's neck.

A terrible shrieking filled the room, as did Laetitia's siblings. Tank flung Laetitia against the far wall, where her body smashed a mirror that had been covered with an old tapestry. She remained pinned to the wall several feet up while shards crashed to the floor. The siblings descended upon the female guest, pushing and shoving away at one another. None of them got enough. They lifted themselves from the body and veered toward Laetitia.

"What THE FUCK?!" screamed Tammy and Tracy.

Tank muscled the twins back and grabbed Laetitia by the throat. "Yeah," he said, seething with anger. "What the fuck, Tish? You've screwed this whole thing up. Those two are all over social media. They will have checked in here, tagged this, dropped a pin here, and Jesus Christ you have so BLOWN THIS!" He left her fall to the floor and raked his mop-like hair with the thick fingers of both of his hands.

"Where's ... Todd ..." breathed Laetitia.

"Where do you think?" roared Tank. Behind him, the twins were piercing the male on the ankles, wrists, and stomach. "He totally freaked when you started this scene. God knows where he is."

Post-feed, Laetitia had regained colour, composure, and a sense of sadness that she had not known since the death of her parents. She surveyed the destroyed dining room and the skewed wedding portrait. She looked down at the dead young couple, whose only ambition was to have an adventure that was, in its ridiculous ignorance, completely in line with the upbringing of millions of others their own age. It was all they knew. She had taken their last moments. She had shown them hell.

"I need to die," she said quietly, overflowing with guilt and certainty.

"Sure as fuck you do!" hissed Tracy, who wheeled from the body and smashed Laetitia's head against the wall, holding her there. Tank stood quietly. Laetitia acknowledged Tank's agreement through his passivity. She'd lost him. She lowered her head and began to sob.

"No," said Tammy.

Tammy had been jealous of Laetitia since her birth. Unlike her twin, Tammy was not athletic, artistic, or helpful. Her only claim to fame in school had been that of the "easy" twin. Still, being identical to Tracy in appearance had made for automatic attendance of social events for Tammy, thus diverting a powerful river of envy and hatred away from Tracy downstream and in the direction of the youngest sibling.

"She lives," proclaimed Tammy, with a sudden and unprecedented confidence. In a completely unforeseen moment of triumph, she had decided the fate of her perpetually younger, smarter, friendlier, prettier sister. Tammy knew she had the backing of the siblings. "She lives, and she suffers. Quite the mess she's got to clean up when the families of these poor shits get here, yeah?" She grinned, a distorted shadow of their mother in the oddly angled portrait behind her.

Tracy released her grip on Laetitia, who dropped in a misshapen pile to the floor.

"Let's get outta here," Tammy said to Tank and Tracy, pointing toward the front door. "I don't know about you, but I'm fucking hungry."

Laetitia did not watch them leave. She didn't have to; she felt the energy of what had been left of her family disappear from the farmhouse. She sat with the two bodies as the sun rose. She did not register that her siblings would have gone to bed. She did not register anything.

In Fall

The clicks of industrial light switches snapped to the ON position echoed around and around the large room. The sound bounced off glass and tile, expanding into a long fade as the glow of overhead lights began to fill the space. Kait's nose and skin registered the chlorine in the air, then forgot it. Her breathing was deliberate and metered as she climbed the stairs and then more stairs, in the same pattern and sequence she had climbed them thousands of times before. When there were no more stairs, there was the 10m diving platform.

She walked casually midway out onto the platform and looked at nothing. She was surrounded by a relatively new aquatic complex. She did not register its stunning, colourful murals of abstract art; the earliest light of sunrise beyond the glass wall opposite her; or the absolute stillness of the two pools far beneath her. Her tall, athletic, 17-year-old form, wrapped perfectly in a competitive swimsuit, walked off the edge of the platform and into a structureless free fall. The random body shape broke the water and the silence with a startling crash-like sound instead of a splash. It took some time before she surfaced and silkenly pulled herself from the pool. She repeated the climbing and falling procedure twice more.

At the top of the fourth climb, she paused at the end of the platform, stood straight, and raised her arms in posture for a rehearsed dive. Then she fell forward in a Jesus Christ pose, and used the entirety of the fall's duration to rotate her body 180 degrees backward in time for a flawless entry. As per the previous maneuvers, she remained underwater for an extraordinary length of time. She surfaced at the edge of the pool under the boards to meet her coach.

"Ready, Freddy?" he asked, his tone light, his face intense.

Kait nodded as she exited the water and began to climb again. "Let's do this."

Later that afternoon, during Monday's sixth-period geography class, Kait's phone lit up in her desk with a text. She looked down from the lesson.

Mel

SNOTBALL <<

Kait choked and then coughed her way through the stares of her teacher and classmates. Upon regaining control, she waved to the room and found a strained semblance of her voice. "I'm OK. Sorry."

Some of the looks lingered. Kait was a quiet, model student. She feigned normalcy until heads turned to the front of the class and regular instruction resumed. She subtly reached for her phone and responded to her little sister, who had adopted a pattern of sending childlike texts such as this as Kait's competition dates approached.

>> Seriously.

u need to lighten up party this weekend @owens <<

>> Please stop hanging around him. You know I dumped him for a reason. Also it's Monday. I didn't see you today are you even here?

sure also I'm lying <<

>> Sooo predictable. See you on the bus?

maybe bye snoreface <<

I hate that she hangs with Owen, thought Kait, her brow furrowed. Talking to her sister about this had been predictably pointless. Kait put her head in one hand and pretended to take some notes with the other. That's great, she thought. Now I get to think about this party all week. With that, the bell rang, signaling the end of the school day and her train of thought.

She checked her phone as she flowed through the student melee in the hallway. Other texts had included one from her boyfriend. Mac was three years her senior and frequently wanting to go out for pizza, the timing of which always seemed to coincide with a test the next morning. She declined the offer. With diving three mornings a week and on weekends, plus gymnastics and other training on alternate evenings of the week, she was used to declining offers. The invitations still mattered. They were a reassurance that the rest of her life was still out there, even if it was largely going by without her.

On the bus ride home in the sharp, late-day sunlight of early fall, Kait's sister was unsurprisingly absent. Kait chatted with her friends, who were actively discussing procrastination tactics for the evening. They all disliked Grade 12 math. They all disliked their teacher, except one girl who was really drawn to older men with thinning hair and bad glasses. This view was shared by no one.

"See ya," came the chorus of girls as Kait descended the steps of the bus and headed up the driveway to her home. She took a couple of deliberate breaths before entering the small bungalow.

It took a familiar, determined length of time for Kait's vision to adjust to the darkness of the entryway once she had closed the front door behind her. It took a familiar, determined length of time for the sensations hitting her eyes and nose and lungs to adjust to the remnants of thousands of cigarettes, recent and distant. The silhouette of her mother's head and neck was one with the armchair, backlit by the bright screen of the television and its late afternoon programming. Judge Judy. Dr. Phil. The living room curtains were drawn and unmoving, as they had been for the past six years. Between the curtains and the chair stood a floor model ashtray straight out of the late 1960s, above which Kate's mother's hand and forearm were suspended, also in silhouette. A cigarette was balanced between her fingers, above which a line of smoke rose straight toward the ceiling without disturbance. It fluttered slightly as the movement of the front door reached it.

"Hi," said Kait, heading straight to the kitchen, whose environment benefitted from a lack of curtain over the small window above the sink. She began to rinse out her lunch dishes in natural light.

"Hello, Kaitlyn. Good day?" asked her mother.

"Yeah."

"Good practice?"

"Awesome. I was really happy with it today."

"Good. Where is your sister?"

"Dunno."

This after-school conversation was fairly standard. It was followed by the standard grunt of disapproval from the living room.

Kait filled the dishwasher with her own Tupperware and then cleaned up whatever her mother had left strewn about the kitchen that day. She paused in the hallway where the kitchen and living room intersected, directing her voice toward the back of everything. "Math test tomorrow. Going to study until supper, OK?"

"Sure."

Moving down the hallway, which became darker with every step on account of all the closed doors, Kait paused in front of Mel's room. She gently pushed the door open into complete darkness, and heard the sound of her sister's sleep-heavy breathing. Kait closed the door carefully and crossed the hall to the bathroom.

The bathroom offered a functional degree of daylight. She opened a large, airtight plastic container and pulled out two large towels. She ran water in the bathtub, soaked the towels thoroughly, and rang them out. She carried the first one to her sister's door, knelt down, and placed it along the bottom of the doorway. She carried the other to her own room and bent to remove the towel she had placed when she had left for school that morning. She darted inside and shut the door immediately behind her. She turned and dropped the second wet towel, pushing it tightly into the crevice, blocking off any chance of the toxic cigarette air coming in.

Her eyes adjusted again, this time to her small but wonderful sanctuary. She had painted the walls a bright yellow. Her bedspread, desk, and shelves were a majestic dark blue. The silver and gold of her diving trophies and medals, lined up precisely on the top two shelves, shone bright and strong against their blue platform. The room was bright, clean, and impeccably organized. There were no coverings over the window, which remained open year-round.

Kait transferred books from her knapsack to her desk. Her phone signaled a text just as she sat to begin studying. She pulled her phone from the pouch of her hoodie.

Mac

Sucks you're not here <<
...photo.jpg<<

A photo expanded of Kait's boyfriend, a really good-looking, well-dressed young man wearing a deliberate sad face, holding up a pizza whose toppings he had arranged to make an even sadder face.

>>Just under two weeks. Then I can eat and do allll
the things for a little bit. Can't wait! Miss you.

Twelve days was the actual time frame. Twelve days until national Junior Elites, which were being held at her home pool. In her hometown. In a meet that would determine whether she would be accepted to a school in the States with a highly competitive diving program. In a meet that could mean freedom.

Kait's focus was gone from studying. She sighed and looked up at the vertical line of pictures that hung on her wall between the desk and shelves. Up top, a snap of her family at a backyard BBQ eight years ago, when her father was still alive and her mother went outside voluntarily. The middle image, her podium finish at last year's nationals, where she was laughing hysterically at something outside of frame. Below, enveloped from behind by Mac's long arms as they stood at the scenic summit of a hill they had climbed in late August. She suddenly felt stalled and anxious, unsure whether she was looking at her past or at her future. The feeling lingered as she turned back toward her math books and began to flip through one of them. Before she knew it, she was fully engrossed in study, the unsettledness gone. The sun had moved across the wall to the column of pictures, reflecting only itself in the glass.

"Well, I think that's a wrap!" Marco's hand hit the table with enthusiasm. He almost leaped from his chair. "This is so exciting!" He leaned in closer to Kait. "Are you excited or what?"

Kait couldn't help but smile at Marco's enthusiasm. He was the head of University of South Carolina's international recruiting department. His job was to be excited. It was a natural fit, as excitement seemed to come easily to him. He was Mac's age. She had been in correspondence with him for the better part of a year, and was still somewhat taken aback by the unfailing positivity. "Of course I am," she said. "For a whole lot of things. Starting with Saturday, obviously."

Kait's morning training sequence consisted of her unusual yet consistent free-fall warm up, followed by practice, followed by her team meeting. Marco had joined the team soon after he had been in correspondence with Kait and her coach, and after she had made a few headlines nationally. He had become a regular feature over the past few months.

The remainder of the team sitting around the table nodded in unison. This consisted of her coach, Jamie; her trainer, Nadia; and the high school's athletic director, Mr. Sanderson. Mr. Sanderson was still trying to get used to the public profile that Kait had built over the past three years, as well as the attention that went with it. It was nothing he had ever experienced as a mid-level athlete, or as a bored and boring physical education teacher, or as the guy who was awarded the athletic director position by default on account of the number of applicants, which had totaled zero. He didn't mind the extra money, though. Meanwhile, the Kait Train had exposed him to all sorts of stimulation and nerves he had never invited or imagined. The media interviews were the worst, especially when he had to do them with Kait. She had come along much better in their joint media training sessions.

Marco's pure white smile sprang from his dark features, a combination of Italian American genetics and southern U.S. tan. "Your mom coming on Saturday?"

All heads lowered except Kait's and Jamie's. "Nah," replied Kait, with what had become a casual effortlessness over time and repetition. "Probably not."

"I'll come by later and see what I can do. She finds me fun."

"This is true," said Kait.

Indeed, on his first visit to the house, Marco had sauntered in as if it was any other home, any other living room, with any other chain-smoking mother quagmired in grief further compounded by a convoluted family history of her own — any and all of which she literally couldn't stand to have illuminated. He had spent hours with her. He had made her laugh more than anyone Kait could recall, including her father. While Kait's mother was fairly mobile within the house and still looked after the family's meals, Marco had cooked up a storm and waited on her hand and foot.

"We'll see," Kait continued. "I'm not expecting a revolution." She made eye contact with Jamie, and did the same with Nadia once she raised her head. "We don't need to work it into my rehearsal."

Nadia seemed visibly comforted by this statement. Her family had been close to Kait's father's family for years. She was unable to wrap her head around how Kait had compartmentalized so much at such a young age, and had risen from the crowd to become the country's top junior diver, about to nail down a full scholarship and a ticket to international and Olympic competition. Nadia had been to Kait's home only once in the last five years. She couldn't cope with the cloud of depression that hung over it any more than she could stomach the haze of cigarette smoke. "We'll work on twists for the rest of the week," she said. "As insurance, of course," she added with a wink and a smile.

The group allowed itself a light laugh. They rose one by one. "See you all tomorrow!" sang Marco. He bounced from the room first. When it was only Jamie and Kait remaining, Jamie closed the door again. Despite efforts to maintain an appearance of steeled intensity at all times, his face now softened. It took Kait aback briefly. "Is there actually any chance she'll show?" he asked gently. "This is different, Kait."

"But it's not," she replied, mildly puzzled, shaking her head. "It won't matter who is in the stands. It never does."

Jamie nodded. "Ok. If it becomes anything else for you – anything at all – just say. We'll work it in."

"Great," said Kait. The room was suddenly claustrophobic to her. She slid her backpack up and over her shoulders and stood beside the door. Jamie didn't move. "We good?" she asked. The grown-up needs reassurance, she realized. She had reached for the doorknob, but then paused and withdrew her hand. "I think you're more nervous than me, Jameson," she said with a smile.

This broke his tension. He let himself smile a little. "This is huge for you, Kait. But you probably know that it's a pretty big deal for all of us, each in our own ways."

She nodded. She was well aware that Jamie and Nadia were living vicariously through her success, neither of them having achieved this level in their own competitive eras. "Of course I know. And I know I wouldn't be here just on my own. No matter what happens, I am so grateful for all of you."

"No matter what happens," laughed Jamie. "We all know what's going to happen." His intensity returned. "Good meeting today, and good work earlier," he said, opening the door. "See you tomorrow."

"Later," she said over her shoulder.

Kait went to class. She did her schoolwork. She found herself more preoccupied by the upcoming competition than usual, but this was par for the course on the week of a meet. She texted back and forth with encouraging friends. When she emerged after school into a downpour, she saw the headlights of a car flashing on and off in the parking lot. It was Mac. Her face filled with a smile and she sprinted for the car.

"What are you doing?" she laughed, pulling the door shut behind her quickly. He immediately leaned over and kissed her.

"This is my last chance to see you before I watch you climb up there on Saturday," he said. He grinned from ear, full of encouragement and pride. "I wanted to tell you face-to-face that you're amazing. And to give you this." He reached behind her to back seat, and returned with a gift-wrapped box. "This is my good luck charm for you."

Mac tended to pay for their day trips and meals out, but, despite his trust fund status, he wasn't much into gifts. This was fine by her. She didn't miss what she had never had. At this moment, she was surprised but also pleased. She pulled the ribbon and opened the box. Nestled in tissue paper was a competitive swimsuit she had been eyeing online for months. It wasn't the colour she had looked at; it was much brighter than what she was used to wearing, and it was stunningly beautiful.

"Will you wear it?" he asked tentatively. "It's as close as I'll get to you until after the meet."

She threw herself into his arms. She felt a pressing from the inside against the walls of her chest. In a delayed reaction, she recognized it as the urge to cry. She instantly stifled it. "It's amazing," she said, pulling back and kissing him. "I can't wait."

Kait emerged from the car and dashed through the rain to her house. She opened the door to the smell of a garlic sauce that nearly overpowered the smell of smoke, along with the sound of Marco and her mother laughing hysterically in the darkness of the living room. "Marco DeLuca, you're bad," drawled her mother.

"What?" he said, allowing the Italian accent to shine through. "I got a mama, too, you know. Hey!" The accent broke, and he rose to greet Kait with a double-cheek kiss.

"Where is your sister?" asked her mother, whose eyes never left Marco as he headed to the kitchen.

Kait watched this with interest. "Dunno," she replied distractedly.

Her mother uncharacteristically whispered. "That guy is fabulous. Mac's nice and everything, but this guy is going places – and he will actually be where you're going. And look at him. Just look at him!" Her tone changed slightly as she caught where her expression was going. "He's COOKING!"

"Oh my God, Mother," exhaled Kait. "I gotta go get changed."

This was a lie. Kait executed the steps of the towel soak / exchange routine on her way down to her room. She discovered that Mel was not in. She felt a brief twinge of concern, but her mind was elsewhere.

Sealed into her room, Kait opened her backpack, which was shiny and wet from the rain. She removed the swimsuit, placed it on a hanger, and hung it from the corner of the top shelf with her trophies. After a moment of watching it swing back and forth, she took it down and turned toward the triptych of photos on the wall. She reached up and hung it on an old, painted-over nail above the photos. The swimsuit covered the photos, and became a work of art in itself.

Friday night was to be an early curfew night. Kait watched a limited amount of television with her mother, which she always did when she was home ahead of a meet. She always wished she could watch more, but the smoke was prohibitive. She said her typical goodnight and felt her phone vibrate in her pocket as she stood. "I'm going out for some air," she said in the direction of her mother's profile in the chair, all the more pronounced by the lack of natural light coming from the kitchen.

"OK," replied her mother's voice.

Kait stepped out the front door and sat on the steps. She smiled in anticipation of a barrage of texts from Mac. Instead:

Mel

OMG he's a fucking JERK<<
I'm really drunk K he's a fucking jerk I should
have listened and I can't get out of here<<

Kait took off in a dead run for Owen's house. She dialed Mac as she ran.

Before daylight, Kait rose and took the swimsuit down lovingly from the forgotten nail high up on the wall. For a second, she wondered what might have once hung from there. She could not remember. In the darkness, the picture frames held three black squares. As she stared at them, her mind was overtaken by a flood of images from the night before. She shook her head, took a deep breath, and turned from her thoughts and the photos to her future.

What a morning it became. The media had been set up at the pool well before Kait began her warm-up routine, and were told to wait. She did four interviews, one accompanied by Mr. Sanderson, who had actually found himself smiling and far more verbose than usual. He occasionally gripped his secret weapon, a travel mug of coffee and Baileys, for reassurance. Marco and his smile were in almost every photo op.

When Kait later emerged from practice for another set of interviews, her entire graduating class, including the football cheerleading squad, had packed the lobby of the aquatic centre. They howled with joy and encouragement. The vast majority of them wore KAIT TRAIN T-shirts. She laughed and laughed as her group of friends emerged wearing swimsuits over top of their street clothing. They proceeded to run around and execute a hopeless version of a synchronized swimming routine.

The last of the PR and greetings over, Kait and her team moved down the back hallway toward the pool area. "Having a good day?" asked Jamie. For the first time since she had known him, he appeared nervous on the day of a meet.

"The best," she replied, knowing that her grin would put him at ease.

They arrived at the door of the dressing room. He paused as if about to break step in their routine. The timing of this was not welcome; she froze briefly in anticipation of the unfamiliar. He gave her the look he always did. "Ready, Freddy?"

She nodded and opened the door. "Let's do this."

Standing in front of the mirror, Kait was slightly taken aback at the magnificence of the swimsuit and her form in it. In her eyes, she saw none of the fatigue that she felt from spending most of last night consoling her younger sister, who had narrowly escaped the disconcerting variety of physical dominance that had instantly put an end to her own time as Owen's girlfriend. Mac had not escaped a black eye. This had been suffered in an altercation with Owen and his friends, which Owen and friends had lost. The frame of the mirror showed her everything she had been working toward for years. Despite, or perhaps because of the last twelve hours, she felt calm.

"Hey!" yelled a competitor behind her, meeting her eyes in the mirror. Kait turned and hugged her friend from a neighbouring province, against whom she had competed steadily and fiercely for the last three years. Despite the pressure and the intensity of the meet, they were thrilled to see each other. The other divers joined in with happiness and encouragement. They all knew it was a big day for Kait. Only one diver didn't participate in the ritual, which, however informal, was not really optional. Kait recognized the girl as her only national competitor for the spot at USC. Despite the invitation for cattiness, nothing was said, and the competition started.

In the arena, the cheerleaders performed routines while sweating profusely in the humid pool environment. There was noise and cheering. There were banners and video cameras. There were scouts from other schools, and there were instant replays. There was a barely contained mass of energy. There was a scoreboard on which Kait was out in front immediately, and for the duration of the meet.

The last round of dives began.

"You've – got – this" mouthed Jamie from the coaches' area. She met his gaze and acknowledged with a brief nod. She tossed her towel and began to climb.

At the top of the climb, she walked toward the edge of the platform as the crowd's collective sound faded in anticipation. She looked straight ahead and saw nothing. Uncharacteristically, she began to feel pressure against the inside of her chest, well aware this time that it was the urge to cry. She had planned for this. It had been part of her mental rehearsal all week, in case this moment suddenly came to her. In case its honesty guided her home.

She reached the edge of the platform, stood straight, and raised her arms. She allowed herself to feel the hope, excitement, and energy of everyone she loved and had loved. Before she burst into tears, she let herself fall forward in the Jesus Christ pose, and executed her signature, final warm-up dive with an unprecedented level of grace and perfection.

As she slid into the water below, the cognizant portion of the crowd registered shock. The uneducated participants cheered and clapped into a reservoir of emptiness. Among them were Mel and her friends, who had leapt to their feet, screaming, "WOOOOOO!" The crowd began to murmur in its confusion.

In the coaches' area, Nadia looked at the scoreboard in disbelief. Jamie was pacing with his head in his hands. "What has she done?" he asked of no one.

"She didn't do the dive," said Mr. Sanderson without thinking.

"I KNOW THAT!" yelled Jamie.

In her choice to disregard her submitted dive, Kait had chosen to discard the win and her scholarship to USC. She altered the path she had been forging every single day since she first stepped off a 10m diving platform. She altered the paths of those on her training team. She altered the paths of everyone close to her.

Underwater, Kait floated, her arms and legs stretched out wide. The pressure in her chest returned suddenly, and she wondered if she would make it back to the surface. Part of her ached terribly from the immense and untended hurt of the past; another felt overwhelming guilt about the consequences of her decision for her people above water. The pressure subsided, buying her some sense of relief and a little more time before she would need to surface. She knew she would emerge from the pool to a world entirely changed from what she had known. The calm that filled her body was not unfamiliar, yet it was completely different somehow. All of her being welcomed it.

Reactions above water were gracious but mixed. The crowd gave her full acknowledgement, their noise and cheering fueled by her gracious and visibly heartfelt acknowledgement of them. She redirected their appreciation to the dark-haired, shy scholarship winner, who had achieved the impossible by way of Kait's last zero score. Marco was nowhere to be found. Jamie did his best, although he was visibly shaken. Nadia gave her a long hug that had nothing to do with her role as trainer. Mr. Sanderson was unsure as to what to do, so he shook Kait's hand for too long before promptly leaving the building. Finally, she left the dressing room, dressed in her hoodie and sweatpants instead of her team uniform. She walked across the empty lobby to Mac.

Even though it was difficult, she held his gaze. She saw his confusion, his pride, his disappointment, his uncertainty about their future. His caring. His black eye.

"I have so many questions," he said, with all honesty.

"I'm sure you do," she replied.

He looked around and then down to his hands, one of which was clutching his car keys with visible tension. He saw this and relaxed his grip. "What do we do now?"

"We go for pizza," she said.

"We could have done that if you'd won."

She shook her head and took his free hand. "It wouldn't have been the same."

Acknowledgements

How many people read this part of a book? I usually skip it. But now, having written a book, I fully understand why this section exists, and how important it is.

The professional writers who agreed to provide early feedback for my stories were Alison Lawrence and Allan Cooper. The grace, encouragement, and quality of information received were invaluable to the completion of this work, and to my growth as an emerging writer. Reaching out to them was among the best artistic decisions I have ever made.

Three friends kindly accepted to read the manuscript and provide feedback. Loretta Hawley-McAleer, Eric Lewis, and Rhonda Whittaker are strong writers in their respective fields. From the breadth of their collective experience, their thoughts and reactions helped to bring my stories to life beyond what I was capable of doing alone. Their technical comments were tremendously helpful. Other comments sparked debate about language, ethics, and characters. The three of you were deliberately chosen. I hope you know how much it meant to me that you accepted.

Along with some amazing observations and suggestions, Rhonda Whittaker provided copy editing. I discovered that this is akin to the mastering process for audio recordings. The overall quality of my book is much better for the breadth and depth of her contribution.

My parents might find this book challenging. But I acknowledge them here, because I love them. And because they are inevitably represented in some manner or other in here. They can choose where.

What may come of my darkness is lifelong question. Its outcomes vary with our trajectory, sometimes instant by instant. As this publication emerges into light, I am filled with gratitude for the light I share with Michelle Jay, and for her trust in our joy.

About the Author

Robin Anne Ettles was born in Edmonton, AB and grew up in a number of Canadian provinces. She completed master's level psychology studies à l'Université de Moncton. She also had a good run as a professional touring musician and songwriter, and continues to play. Her current province of residence  is Prince Edward Island, where she is close to the beach, her family, her chosen family, and good food and drink.

This is her first book.

www.ingramcontent.com/pod-product-compliance
Lightning Source LLC
Chambersburg PA
CBHW051255170626
46809CB00004B/1658